ChangelingPress.com

Blossom Creek Duet

Contemporary Women's Fiction

Paige Warren

Blossom Creek Duet

Contemporary Women's Fiction

Paige Warren

ISBN: 978-1-60521-870-0

Publisher:
Changeling Press LLC
315 N. Centre St.
Martinsburg, WV 25404
ChangelingPress.com

Printed in the U.S.A.

Editor: Crystal Esau
Cover Artist: Bryan Keller

The individual stories in this anthology have been previously released in E-Book format.

Table of Contents

Valentina's Miracle (Blossom Creek 1)
Paige Warren

Valentina Cupid has always despised her name and the stupid holiday that goes with it. Starting over in the small town of Blossom Creek, she's hoping for a miracle. Down to her last few dollars, she has no choice but to sleep in the car with her two kids, hoping to blend in with the other cars parked at Gleason Auto. But one sexy mechanic definitely notices.

Jesse Jameson is no one's idea of a knight in shining armor. With a checkered past and a trail of broken hearts, he's not anyone's ideal. Still, when he sees the single mom sleeping in her car, he knows he can't just walk away. But Jesse underestimates the temptation that is Valentina Cupid, and one kiss ignites a passion that won't be denied. He's going to prove to Valentina he's not like her loser exes, and he's going to give her a Valentine's Day to remember.

Chapter One

Valentina Cupid tried to ease the tension in her neck. Her children, Max and Katy, were asleep in the backseat. It had only been a few days since Gage had walked out of their lives, or more like run. Valentina had come home to find his things packed and gone, and an eviction notice tacked to the door. She'd quietly packed their belongings, put the kids in the car, and just drove until her vision blurred. After travelling for three days, she was down to their last hundred dollars and knew they couldn't run any further. Blossom Creek, Texas would have to do until she could find a job and earn some more money.

Her hand smoothed over her still flat stomach. At least she wasn't showing yet. A new start in a new town was just what her little family needed, but she knew once people learned her kids all had different fathers, they'd sneer at her just like the last town had done. She had a thing for bad boys who knocked her up and took off, and never seemed to learn her lesson. If she ever dated again, she'd have to pick a nice, nerdy guy who sat at a desk every day. Tattoos and muscles were overrated.

"Momma, I'm hungry," Max said from the backseat.

The box of peanut butter crackers lay empty on the passenger seat. She'd bought it yesterday in hopes of spreading their cash a little further, but her kids really needed a hot meal. A diner on the right caught her attention and she pulled into a space out front. Scrubbing her hands up and down her face a few times, she unbuckled her seatbelt and got the kids out of their car seats. They'd been travelling for three days, only stopping at truck stops and rest areas long enough for Valentina to close her eyes for an hour here and there.

She gripped their hands as they entered the diner and waited to be seated. It seemed almost as if every eye in the place turned their way. Valentina's cheeks flushed and she tried to avoid their gazes. An older woman wearing an apron came over, flashing them a smile.

"You want a table or a booth?" the waitress asked.

Max tugged on her hand. "Can we have a booth, Momma?"

The waitress nodded. "I know just the spot."

She grabbed a menu and three rolls of silverware before leading the way to a booth in the window. Max and Katy both needed booster seats, but once they were settled, Valentina slid into the other side. She was so damn tired the words on the menu ran together and turned into black fuzzy blotches, but she fought to focus and remain upright. Her kids needed her.

She read off the menu choices they could afford and let Max pick his meal. Katy hardly ever ate anything but mashed potatoes and mac 'n cheese. As much as Valentina wanted to order the biggest burger with the largest order of fries on the menu, she settled for a cup of soup and some crackers. After she placed their order, the waitress returned with some paper and crayons for the kids.

"Thought they might want something to do while you wait for your food," the woman said. "I'm Barb. Just holler if you need anything."

"Thank you," Valentina said with a tired smile.

When their food was delivered, Barb set down a large salad with chunks of grilled chicken and a side of ranch. Valentina opened her mouth to protest that she hadn't ordered it when the woman held up a hand.

"You need more than soup," Barb said. "Won't do your kids any good if you pass out from hunger."

Valentina's cheeks flushed.

"You sticking around town or passing through?" Barb asked.

"I thought we'd stay for a while."

"Diner's closing in an hour. Why don't you wait until the customers are gone, and if you'd like, you can help me close up. I'll pay you cash."

Valentina's face burned with embarrassment as she nodded in agreement. Was it noticeable that they were on their last leg? She hated accepting charity, but if Barb would let her work for the salad and a few extra dollars to get them by a little longer, she couldn't say no. They ate their food and the kids colored a little more while they waited for the diner to empty. When the last customer had walked out, Barb locked the door and flipped the sign to *Closed*.

"You ever worked in a diner before?" Barb asked.

"Yes, ma'am."

Barb snorted. "None of that ma'am nonsense. Just call me Barb. I'm going to let you refill the napkins and condiments at each table. Then you can sweep and mop the floor. I'll be in the kitchen helping Hank prep for tomorrow. Come on. I'll show you where everything is."

It took almost two hours for Valentina to get everything done, and her kids had fallen asleep at the table by the time she was finished. Barb insisted on paying her twenty dollars in addition to the salad she'd already provided, and wouldn't take no for an answer. Valentina pocketed the money and carried her kids to the car one at a time, fastening them back into their car seats. She had no idea where they'd go for the night, but fatigue pulled at her.

Valentina drove until she found a darkened parking lot by a large building marked Gleason Auto. It seemed to be closed for the night, and she hoped to blend in with the other cars in the lot waiting for repairs. She turned off her headlights and shut off the engine. She'd have to wake in an hour and run it again to warm the car back up, but she didn't have enough gas to leave it running all night.

She reclined her seat a little and closed her eyes, after making sure the doors were all locked and the windows all the way up. Her body felt like lead weights were pulling her down and her eyes burned from exhaustion. She knew pushing herself so hard wasn't good for the baby, but she had little choice right now. Barb hadn't mentioned a permanent position tonight, which meant Valentina would have to spend some of her money on a local paper and see if any jobs were posted. It was that or walk up and down the main strip checking with every store along the way. Not that she had any idea what she'd do with her kids while she worked. She couldn't afford daycare without a job, but she couldn't work without someone to watch the kids.

Valentina let sleep pull her down, sleeping harder than she had in days. A slight chill in the air woke her a while later. Valentina looked into the backseat, and her heart lurched when she saw how flushed Katy looked. Her daughter had kicked off her blanket at some point and shivered in her car seat. Max still dozed, but looked fine. Valentina got out of the car and opened the back door. Katy was burning with fever, but Max felt cool to the touch. Her heart ached as she realized her heavy sleeping had likely gotten her child sick, since she hadn't been awake to turn the heat back on, all because she couldn't afford a motel room.

Booted steps came toward her and she spun to face the person, her hand at her throat as her heart raced. A man, who didn't look much older than her twenty-two years had a scowl on his face as he approached. Despite the cold February air, his short sleeve shirt displayed the tattoos on his arms. The man drew nearer and brushed his long hair out of his face.

"This is private property," he said, his deep voice sending shivers down her spine.

Not another bad boy, Valentina. Get a grip. "I'm sorry. I didn't realize we were trespassing."

"We?" he asked as he came to a stop in front of her. The man peered around her shoulder and his eyes widened a little when he saw her kids in the backseat. "Holy shit. Did you sleep in your car last night?"

Valentina's cheeks burned. "Yes."

"Bring the kids inside and warm them up," he said, turning to head toward Gleason Auto. "I have some hot chocolate they can drink."

She bit her lip. "Is there a free clinic in town?"

He paused and turned to face her again. "A free clinic?"

"My daughter. I think she's sick."

The man came closer again, peering into the backseat. "Blossom Creek doesn't have a free clinic. Do you not have insurance?"

"No, we don't."

"Old Doc Johnson owes me a favor. Bring your kids inside and I'll have him stop by on his way to his office this morning. The three of you can get warm while you wait."

"I don't even know you. Why are you helping us?" Valentina asked.

"Let's just say I have a soft spot for kids. Why isn't your husband here helping you?"

"I'm not married," she said softly.

"And their dad?"

"Max's dad left two years ago. Katy's dad took off right after I told him I was pregnant."

"Two different dads?" he asked, his eyebrows lifted.

Valentina placed a hand on her stomach. "Three."

He studied her a moment and seemed to come to some sort of decision. "You need help getting the kids inside?"

"You're still going to help us?"

"Figure someone should. Sounds like you're the type to attract assholes."

Valentina bit her lip. He wasn't wrong.

"My name's Jesse Jameson, almost like the outlaw, and I promise you and the kids are safe with me."

"Valentina Cupid, and my kids are Max and Katy."

Jesse motioned to the car. "Want some help?"

She nodded hesitantly and unbuckled Max first. Her gaze never left Jesse as he carefully lifted her son out of the car seat, then she unbuckled Katy and pulled her out too. Grabbing her keys from the ignition, she locked the car and followed Jesse into the auto place. He led her into the back where there was a large break room that held a couch, TV, and a small table with four chairs, along with a kitchenette.

Max rubbed his eyes as Jesse set him down on the couch and her son looked around in curiosity. Valentina eased Katy down next to her brother before facing Jesse again.

"Hot chocolate for the kids? Are they too young?" he asked.

"Max has had it before, at room temperature, but Katy is still too small. She's only eighteen months old. If you could watch them just long enough for me to grab their bag from the car, they both have sippy cups. If you have some juice or milk, I could give them that."

He nodded. "Go ahead. I'll see what's in the fridge."

Valentina rushed outside and grabbed the kids' bag from the passenger seat of her car, then hurried back inside. She didn't know why she'd trusted him with her kids, but there was something about Jesse that made her feel safe. When she got back to the break room, Jesse had pulled out a half gallon of milk and a carton of orange juice.

"Both of these are still good," he said.

Valentina rinsed out the sippy cups and filled both with milk, even though she worried about giving her daughter milk if she was sick. She didn't have any Pedialyte, but she knew she'd need to pick some up soon. Except it was supposed to be refrigerated once it was opened, and she didn't exactly keep a fridge in her car.

Once her children were situated, Jesse pulled her aside. "I want you to be honest with me," Jesse said. "Just how much trouble are you in?"

Valentina wasn't sure how much she should tell him. Even though he was helping them, he was still a stranger. Her gaze strayed to her children. She would do anything for them. Even put her trust in the man standing in front of her. She only hoped it wasn't the wrong choice.

* * *

Jesse waited patiently for the woman to respond.

It was obvious she wasn't doing so well, if she was sleeping in parking lots with her kids. She didn't look old enough to be a mom three times over, much less have all three dads run out on her. He tried not to judge people, and figured there was a good reason she was in her current predicament. He'd been judged his entire life and wasn't about to start throwing stones.

"I have just under a hundred dollars left in my purse. Gage wiped out the checking account before he skipped out on us. The only money I had access to were my tips that I'd hidden and had been saving since Christmas." She shrugged. "I'd thought he was different, but then they never are. I guess I have a type."

"Deadbeat assholes?" Jesse asked.

Valentina gave a humorless laugh. "Yeah, that about sums it up. I've always had a thing for bad boys, and I guess it just hasn't really worked out so well for me."

Jesse grinned a little. He'd been called a bad boy often enough, but these days he was a law-abiding citizen. He wondered how many hearts he'd broken getting to this point though. As far as he knew, he'd never fathered a child, and if he had, that was definitely something he'd want to know. Having grown up in the system, he couldn't think of anything worse than abandoning your kid.

He could help Valentina, and her kids, if she'd let him. But they were strangers, and after she'd been burned three times by guys like him, how likely was she to accept his help? She had come into the shop with him, and they were waiting for Doc Johnson, but once her daughter was treated how fast would she run out of here? And where would she go? "Do you have a plan?" he asked.

"I'd thought I'd get a paper today and check the employment section, see if I could find a job."

"And what are you doing with them while you work?" he asked, nodding his head toward the kids, who had fallen back asleep on the couch.

"I don't know. Maybe I could find a job where they could go with me. Delivering papers or something?"

"Newspaper's owned by the Richmond family and they only hire family." Jesse folded his arms across his chest. "What kind of work experience do you have?"

"Mostly waitressing. I answered phones for a short time at a dental office, but my kids kept getting sick and they let me go when I called in one too many times."

"Any good with computers? Like entering client data?" Jesse asked.

"I could probably do that if someone showed me how to use the program. I was pretty good with computers in high school, but I haven't had access to one since then unless I use one at the library."

Would she see his offer as charity? His shop had been turning a nice profit the last two years, and since he slept in the apartment upstairs and owned the building outright, he didn't have a lot of expenses. He could easily afford to hire someone to help out.

"Do you know of something?" she asked. "I promise I'm a hard worker. I just need someone to give me a chance."

"I need someone to handle the front desk here. I haven't put an ad in the paper yet, but if you accept the position you'll save me the trouble of advertising. It's mostly answering phones and greeting clients. You'll need to keep the coffee pot full in the waiting room and keep everything clean. There will be some data entry and you'll accept payments."

Her eyes widened. "You're offering me a job?"

Jesse shrugged. "I need someone and you're looking, so why not?"

"You don't know anything about me."

"I know you need help, and I'm willing to give it to you. The question is whether or not you'll accept it. The pay isn't great, but I can offer you eight dollars an hour. Full-time employees are eligible for the health plan too. My mechanics get five vacation days and a week of sick time every year. No reason you can't have the same."

"You're offering a stranger a full-time job, with benefits, and higher than minimum wage?" she asked, looking skeptical.

"There's room behind the front counter for you to set up a play area for the kids. You could bring them with you, at least until we see how it goes. If they're too disruptive, maybe by that point you'll have enough money set aside to put them in daycare."

Valentina looked from him to her kids then back again. There was indecision in her eyes, but he knew she needed this opportunity, and she'd likely accept for her kids' sake if nothing else. She chewed on her bottom lip and he waited for her to make a decision. He didn't see what choice she had but to accept his offer. He knew the jobs around town were scarce, and none would let her keep her kids with her, even temporarily.

Before she could respond, Doc Johnson appeared in the doorway, an old-fashioned black bag clutched in his hand. He gave Jesse a warm smile before looking at Valentina in curiosity. "I hear I have a new patient," Doc said.

"It's my daughter, Katy," Valentina said. "She's eighteen months old and I think she has a fever."

Doc ambled over to the couch and began pulling things out of his bag. While the little girl slept, he checked her heart and lungs, took her temperature, and attempted to look at her throat. He didn't say much as he studied his patient and Jesse hoped it wasn't anything serious. Doc got the child's full name and date of birth, then scribbled something on a prescription pad and handed it to Valentina.

"Seems to be a common cold, but she does have a fever. You should keep fluids in her and keep her warm. I'd imagine she'll be back to playing in a few days. If she's still doing poorly, give me a call and I'll take another look. Her throat is a little irritated, but not enough for me to think it's strep," Doc said.

"Thank you." Valentina accepted the prescription and looked at it like she didn't have a clue what to do with it. If she hadn't been able to afford a doctor, Jesse figured there was no way she could afford to fill that either.

Doc clapped him on the shoulder and motioned for him to follow him out.

"I'll be back in a minute," Jesse told Valentina.

When they got near the front door, far enough away that Valentina couldn't hear them, Doc sighed heavily. "How much trouble is that young woman in?" he asked.

"She's told me some of it. Basically, she's out of money, has nowhere to stay, and I found her sleeping in her car in my parking lot. I think the little girl took sick overnight because of how cold it was. The car wasn't running when I found them."

"They can't sleep in the car again, Jesse. That little girl needs to be kept warm and comfortable. I expect she'll start coughing later today. That's a good thing. The cough syrup I prescribed will help clear her chest and keep mucus from settling in her lungs. But only if she takes it."

"I'll see that she gets the prescription filled," Jesse said. "And I'll try to convince them to stay with me. They can use my spare bedroom. Not like anyone else ever uses it anyway."

Doc clapped him on the shoulder again and ambled out the door to his waiting car. Jesse ran a hand through his hair as he tried to decide how best to handle the situation with Valentina. She didn't seem like the type who would accept a handout, but maybe he could convince her it was in the best interest of her children.

When Jesse stepped back inside the break room, Valentina was staring at her children with tears in her eyes. He cleared his throat so she'd know she wasn't alone anymore and she quickly dashed at her eyes with both hands. He could only imagine the strain she was under, trying to provide for two kids while pregnant, jobless, and homeless. And if he could ease some of her burden, he was going to. Hopefully, she'd accept the job he'd offered her. With a little luck, maybe he could convince her to sleep in his spare room.

"I should wake up the children so we can get out of your way," she said.

"Leave them," Jesse said. He held out his hand. "Give me the prescription."

"No, you've done enough already."

"If you pay for that prescription, how are you going to pay to feed your kids?"

Her shoulders sagged in defeat. "I don't know."

"We need to talk, but first, you're going to give me that prescription and I'm going to drop it by the pharmacy and arrange to have it delivered here when it's ready. Then we're going to do something about breakfast for the four of us."

"You don't have to feed us too," she said. "You've already arranged for a doctor to see Katy and you're getting her medicine. I can't ask you to do more than that. You've already done too much."

"Valentina, I get the feeling you could use a friend about now. Let me help you. Maybe if someone had been around to help my mom when I was a kid, my life would have turned out differently. So let me do this."

Her gaze turned curious. "You seem to have turned out okay."

"There's a lot you don't know about me, but you're bound to hear it if you work here. We'll talk about it later. I want to be completely honest with you about everything, but right now, my priority is taking care of you and those kids."

She nodded, looking like she wanted to believe him, and yet was too scared to hope that things might be changing for her. Jesse took the prescription, made sure the door to the shop was locked, and he climbed into his truck and drove toward the other end of town. At the pharmacy, old Mr. Worthers stared at the prescription before looking up at Jesse again.

"I don't recall anyone in town by the name of Katy Cupid."

"The family is new in town," Jesse said. "Can you please have that delivered when it's ready? You can add it to my account. And anything else we might need, like a thermometer, can you throw that in too?"

Mr. Worthers grunted and started scanning the slip into the computer system. Assuming that was all the man needed from him, Jesse stepped away from the counter. Before leaving the pharmacy, he stopped on the toy aisle and picked a pink stuffed bunny for Katy and a brown bear for Max. He also grabbed a few cans of chicken noodle soup from the grocery aisle and some apple juice. He didn't know if Katy would require special fluids, but he wanted her to have a choice other than orange juice or milk.

After he checked out, Jesse put his purchases in his truck and drove to the nearest fast food place to pick up some breakfast sandwiches. He'd have to think of something more nutritious for lunch, but maybe this would be enough to keep them going until then. As he drove back to the shop, he wondered what he was going to do to convince Valentina to give him a chance, to accept his offer of help, once she found out the truth about him. She thought he had his life together, and he did… now. But it had been a long, hard road to get to this point. And people around town weren't soon to forget his past transgressions.

Chapter Two

Valentina had rummaged through the kitchen and found the coffee grounds. She'd cleaned the coffeemaker, which was on the grimy side and looked like it hadn't been cleaned in a month, then set about making a pot of coffee. She didn't drink it much while she was pregnant, but a cup right now would go a long way.

The kids were still sleeping on the couch. She'd gone back to her car, leaving them only long enough to get their blankets, and had made sure to lock the door when she came back in. Obviously, Jesse had locked them in for a reason. Maybe he was worried customers would come in while he was gone, or maybe this part of town wasn't as safe as she'd assumed. The town was so quaint, she had a hard time picturing there being a bad side.

Valentina pulled a coffee cup off the tree on the counter, rinsed it, and then poured herself a cup. She usually put creamer in her coffee, but she didn't know if it was all right to use the one in the fridge, or if it was even still any good. She sipped at the bitter brew and fought the urge to curl up with her children and go to sleep. Even though she'd slept longer last night than she had in days, her body was still exhausted from the long haul from California, and the stress of not knowing what would happen to them now. They'd made it to a new town, but now she had no job -- unless she accepted Jesse's offer -- very little money, and nowhere to live.

She leaned against the counter and closed her eyes a moment, breathing in the aroma of the strong coffee. Her stomach rumbled and reminded her it was time to eat again. If Jesse hadn't found them this morning, she didn't know what would have happened to them. Without a free clinic, there would have been no way for Katy to receive treatment. She felt like the worst mother ever, letting her daughter get sick. If she'd just splurged and gotten a motel room for the night, even if it had wiped out their cash, they'd have been safe and warm for at least one evening.

The bell over the front door jingled and she opened her eyes. She heard a sack crinkle and heavy booted steps come down the hall. She hoped it was Jesse, but she didn't know if anyone else had a key to his shop. Was it even his shop? The sign said Gleason and he'd said his name was Jameson. Maybe he was just a mechanic here, even if he did act like he owned the place. Surely, only an owner would have offered her a job?

Jesse stepped into the break room and held up a large, white paper bag. "I got everyone breakfast. You and I both have a sandwich, but I got the eggs and sausage platter for the kids. I didn't know if they could handle a breakfast sandwich, being so little."

"Max probably could have eaten one, but I don't think Katy is up for it just yet. I'm not even certain she'll feel like eating much."

He nodded. "I have a sack in the car with some stuff for them, including soup for Katy. I'll just leave our food with you and run get it. Are you going to wake the kids or let them sleep longer?"

"I should wake them, but it's been a few days since they slept anywhere other than the backseat. It's the first time they've been able to stretch out and get some decent rest."

"Why don't we sit at the table with our breakfast and talk? When we're done, you can wake them up and decide what you're going to do."

She smiled a little. "You make it sound like you murdered someone and I'm going to run screaming from this place."

"Nothing that bad, but my past isn't squeaky clean."

Whose past was? Valentina was running from her own demons. If she hadn't left home, she might not have lived such a hard life the last five years. But then if she'd stayed, there was no telling what would have happened to her. A fate much worse, she was certain. Besides, she had her babies, and she loved them more than anything, even if their daddies had turned out to be jackasses.

Jesse pulled out two paper plates and set out their sandwiches before joining Valentina at the table. They both sipped on coffee and regarded one another, neither making the first move to have what he considered a needed conversation about his past. If there was anything Valentina knew, it was that your past didn't matter. It was who you were today that counted. And so far, Jesse had been kinder to her than anyone had since she'd left home at the age of seventeen.

"If you stick around town, and people see you're spending time with me, you're going to hear things," Jesse said. "When I was about seven, my mom abandoned me. I spent the next nine years in the foster system, bouncing from one home to another. Some I stayed at for months at a time, others mere days."

Her brow furrowed. "I thought you only got out of foster care when you were eighteen."

"Typically. Unless you get caught boosting cars, then spend the last two years in juvie. When I got out, I had nothing. Well, except my knowledge of cars. Paul Gleason owned this shop and he gave me a break.

There was a small studio apartment upstairs that he let me have as part of my pay, and I had enough cash to cover the basics."

"So, Gleason Auto isn't yours?" she asked.

"Oh, it's mine. Now. Paul apparently had a faulty heart. When it gave out, I learned that he'd left the building to me. I own it free and clear, and even though he'd mismanaged the money for years, overspending because he could never turn anyone away, I've been turning a decent profit the past two years. I'm a law-abiding citizen these days, pay taxes and everything."

"Then why does the town say bad things about you?"

"I was a troubled kid, even before the stint in juvie. I got busted for graffiti, marijuana, and underage drinking on more than one occasion, but the sheriff always gave me a break. Until he just couldn't anymore. When my crimes escalated to grand theft auto, he decided I wouldn't turn my life around unless I had to pay the consequences of my actions. I'd always been kind of wild and I guess he thought if the foster care system was failing me, he'd put me somewhere to learn a lesson."

"And was he right?" Valentina asked.

"Maybe." Jesse grinned a little. "Probably. Juvie wasn't so bad. There were some tough guys, gang members, but it wasn't anything like being sent to real prison. I got a lucky break, and when I got out, I got my G.E.D. and I decided I was going to change. I didn't want to spend my adult years behind bars. I worked hard and didn't break a law except for the occasional speed limit."

"And your life of crime is supposed to scare me away?" she asked.

Jesse shrugged. "I wanted to be upfront and honest with you about my past. I didn't want you to hear it from someone else, especially since kids are involved. I swear I'm not that messed-up kid anymore. I don't even smoke cigarettes, much less pot. I do sometimes have a beer or two after work, but I don't get falling down drunk."

"You're not the only one with a past, Jesse. I left home at seventeen because I didn't feel safe in my own house anymore. I had enough money for bus fare and left my small Iowa town for the big lights of L.A. I had stars in my eyes that were quickly dimmed by reality. Life was harder than I'd anticipated and when I met Max's dad, I thought things were turning around. No one had ever really taken care of me before, not without wanting something in return, not even my parents. So he dazzled me. And then he showed his true colors."

"You were seventeen when you met him?" Jesse asked.

"Yeah, and he was twenty-six. I think he got off on having such a young girlfriend, and if anyone ever asked, I lied and said I was eighteen. I was barely nineteen when I had Max and his dad didn't stick around long after that. I guess I wasn't as much fun with a kid in tow, so he split. I was only single a few months before I met Katy's dad. Max's dad was my longest relationship ever. I think I'm doomed to fail in the love department, or maybe I'm just going about things the wrong way."

"And Katy's dad ditched you when you told him you were pregnant."

She nodded. "She was only a few months old when I met Gage, my last boyfriend, and I thought things would be different. He was a bit awkward around the kids, but I thought he'd learned to enjoy spending time with them, even if I did think he drank and smoked too much. We'd only been together a short time when I discovered he was reporting to a parole officer. He'd been busted for selling drugs."

"And you still stayed with him?" Jesse asked.

"I felt like I didn't have a choice. And as far as I knew, he'd turned his life around, like you did. I wasn't making enough to take care of myself and two kids, and then I found out I was pregnant again. I don't know why he took off. He's known for a month about the new baby, and while he never really seemed excited, he wasn't an ass about it either."

"So I guess I don't seem so bad after dating someone who's done hard time."

She laughed a little. "No, you don't. You pulled your life together and you've obviously become respectable. That's something I'll never have."

He frowned at her. "Why don't you think you're respectable? Because you've been living out of your car?"

Her cheeks flushed. "I was called a lot of names where I lived before here."

"Because of the three kids thing?"

"Because the three kids have three dads. I've been called white trash and a whore. I doubt things will be different here once everyone hears of my background. My son is very open about the fact they have different dads -- Katy thinks every man in my life is her dad -- and they'll talk to anyone who will listen. Well, my son talks, my daughter babbles at them."

"I think the people here might surprise you. It's not like you're the first woman around here to fall for a man's lies, or the first to have kids from different dads. Hell, Beth Ann Parkes had a kid by her uncle, and, while they hauled him off to jail, everyone's been real sympathetic to her and that baby."

Valentina's eyes went wide. "Her uncle got her pregnant?"

"It wasn't consensual. But the point is you aren't the only one with a checkered past in this town. There's my juvie record and run-ins with the law, poor Beth Ann, and old Harvey who lives like a hermit in the woods and gets busted once a month for moonshine. Hell, sweet Barb at the diner has been married and divorced eight times, and no one looks down on her."

She nibbled her lip uncertainly. "You really think we could make a home for ourselves here?"

"I really do. But there's going to be a little more fodder for the gossips, because there's no way in hell I'm letting you live in that car for another night. I renovated the apartment upstairs last year and it now has two bedrooms. I want you and the kids to take the spare room."

She opened her mouth to protest, but he held up a hand.

"It's just until you're back on your feet," Jesse said. "If you're not paying rent or for a motel room, then you can put some money aside and grow a little nest egg to get you started. You can stay as long as you need to. I'm not going to kick you out. And since you'll be working here, the commute will be easy."

"Jesse, it's really sweet of you to offer, but --"

He reached out and placed a finger over her lips. "There are no buts. You're going to take the damn spare room. People may talk, but it won't be long before something else sparks their interest and they'll be off and running on another topic. For now, let me help you. I always wondered if someone had been there to help my mom, whether or not she'd have still given me up. I promise it's not a ploy to get you into bed or anything. Not that you aren't sexy as hell, but I figure you have enough to deal with already."

"I'd never give up my kids."

"You're a fighter. I think that's obvious. But even the strong need a helping hand every now and then. So what do you say? Will you take the job and move into the spare room? The kids will be warm and safe at night. I even have some of those kids' channels on cable if they like watching TV."

Valentina sighed. As much as she wanted to walk away and do things her own way, she knew an opportunity like this one wouldn't come up again. It was probably insane to move in with a guy she'd just met, not that she hadn't done it three other times -- and look how that had turned out -- but he'd been kind to her and seemed to genuinely want to help. Besides, Jesse wasn't even asking her to share his bed. Just his apartment.

"Fine. We'll stay," she said.

Jesse grinned and finished his breakfast. Valentina only hoped she didn't come to regret her decision. Something told her living with Jesse wasn't going to be as easy as he made it sound. But what other choice did she have?

* * *

After Valentina had woken the kids and gotten them fed, he helped her get settled upstairs, carrying their meager belongings into the spare room. There was only one bag for all three of them and a small box that contained some books and toys. His heart broke for them, even though he'd known kids who had less. It just didn't seem right that they'd lost their dads and probably most of their possessions, unless this was how little they'd had to begin with. He wanted to make their lives better, to show them that things could be different this time.

"I forgot that sack downstairs, the one with the soup in it," he said. "I'll be right back. Just make yourselves at home."

When he got downstairs, he waved to the two mechanics who had arrived while he was upstairs. They'd been working for Gleason's since before Jesse owned the place and knew what to do without instructions. In the break room, he picked up the sacks from the pharmacy, but paused a moment. While he thought all three of them would easily fit in the bed in the spare room, he didn't think Katy looked big enough to sleep in a regular bed yet.

He pulled out his phone and stared at it. The only woman he'd ever really talked to that was a mom had practically stalked him. Janie still popped up when he least expected it, trying to get into his pants and get a ring on her finger. For some reason, she'd decided he was ideal daddy material and had been trying to lure him into her trap for the last year. No. No way in hell he was calling Janie for advice on kids.

Instead, he called Mrs. Wilson at the library. She knew everyone in town, and was always in everyone's business. But she'd also raised three children and had nine grandchildren. If anyone could help him, it would be Mrs. Wilson. It was still early and the library didn't open for another hour, but he knew she'd be there, probably dusting her precious books.

"Blossom Creek Public Library," she said as she picked up the phone.

"Mrs. Wilson, it's Jesse Jameson. I was hoping you could answer a question or two for me."

"Jesse, the best way to do research is to read. I'm

perfectly aware that you know what a book is."

He chuckled. "Yes, ma'am, but I kind of need the information immediately. What kind of bed would an eighteen-month-old baby sleep in? And can a three-year-old sleep in a regular bed?"

There was silence on the line.

"Does this have anything to do with the stuffed animals you bought at the pharmacy this morning?" she asked.

Damn. He'd thought the rumor mill would hold off for at least a day or two. The curse of small-town living. And he knew once he told Mrs. Wilson he had a woman and two kids living with him, it would spread like wildfire. He'd hoped Valentina would have more time to settle in before the good townspeople stuck their noses in her business.

"Yes, ma'am. I have two kids staying at my place."

"Jesse Jameson, did your wild ways finally catch up to you?"

He nearly choked on his tongue. Jesus. She thought they were *his* kids? "Um, no, ma'am. They've moved in with their momma. They don't have much, just a small box of toys and a bag of clothes. I want the kids to be safe though, and I wasn't sure if it was okay for them to sleep in a regular bed."

"Why didn't you just ask the mother?" Mrs. Wilson asked.

"Because even if the kids did need something, she wouldn't ask me for it. She's proud and stubborn. I just want to make sure the kids are safe in the apartment. I told her she could bring them down to the shop when she's working. I have no idea how to baby-proof my waiting room."

Mrs. Wilson clucked her tongue. "So she's living

with you and working with you?"

He ran a hand through his hair. What the hell did it matter? He just wanted his question answered.

"You're going to need a crib and a toddler bed," Mrs. Wilson said. "And probably a baby gate for your waiting room. You'll need to make sure there aren't exposed outlets wherever the kids will be. Little ones are curious and might stick their fingers in the socket."

"Where do I find all that stuff?" Jesse asked, trying to figure out when in his day he was going to go shopping, and hoping he had enough money to cover everything. But damn if those kids were going to go without.

"Are the children girls or boys?" Mrs. Wilson asked.

Again, what the hell difference did it make? Was she just being nosy?

"The three-year-old is a boy and the eighteen-month-old is a girl."

"As you know, my youngest grandchild is now in first grade. I'll call Mr. Wilson and have him pull out some things we don't need anymore. My children have assured me there will no more babies from any of them so the beds are just collecting dust. You'll need new bedding for them though, and I don't have extra outlet covers."

"I promise we'll take care of the beds and return them as soon as we're able," Jesse said.

Mrs. Wilson tsked. "You keep them as long as you need them, and if they get a little banged up, don't you worry about it. Kids can be rough on their things. As far as I'm concerned, you can keep the beds. I'll have Mr. Wilson look for a baby gate too. We used to have a few of them so I'm sure there's one in the attic somewhere."

"I can't thank you enough, Mrs. Wilson."

"I don't know what's going on, Jesse, why you've hired some single mother and moved her into your place, but I hope this doesn't blow up in your face. Despite your troubled past, you have a good heart. It's easy for people to take advantage of a guy like you."

He smiled a little. "They aren't taking advantage, Mrs. Wilson. I think you'll really like Valentina and her kids. Katy woke up sick this morning, but once she's better I'll make sure I bring them around to meet you."

"See that you do. We have an excellent children's program at the library. I'm sure they would both enjoy it."

"Yes, ma'am."

After Mrs. Wilson hung up, Jesse grabbed the sacks off the counter and carried them upstairs. Valentina was scrubbing the dishes he'd left in the sink last night and Max was trying to play ball with Katy. He smiled as he watched the little boy roll the small rubber ball to his sister, and she batted at it, sending it careening around the room. Max patiently got up to get it and rolled it to her again.

Jesse carried the sacks into the kitchen and set them down on the table. "I hope you don't mind, but I got the kids a little treat at the pharmacy."

She looked at him over her shoulder. "You didn't have to do that."

"I figured they might be a little scared, being in a new place and all. It's just two small stuffed animals. I didn't know if they would like to sleep with them, or if they were even allowed to, but I thought they might be comforting to the kids."

Valentina dried her hands and turned to face him. "So, you took in a pregnant mom with two kids, gave her job, gave them a place to live, called a doctor for her daughter and paid for the prescription, and you bought the kids toys. Are you gunning for sainthood?"

"Not hardly." Jesse smiled. "Is it all right if I give the animals to the kids?"

Valentina peeked into the sacks to look at the animals and then nodded. Jesse grabbed the bear and bunny, then knelt on the floor next to the kids. Both of them were focused on the toys in his hands and had stopped playing ball for the moment. Jesse offered the bunny to Katy and the bear to Max.

"I thought you might want some new friends," he said.

Katy held the bunny tight while Max stared at his for a moment. When the little boy looked up at him, Jesse felt his heart turn over. Chubby little arms closed around his neck as Max hugged him, and then went back to playing with his sister. Even though he hadn't been around them long, he could tell they were good kids. Valentina might have had a rough road to travel, but she'd obviously raised her kids right.

Jesse stood and looked around his apartment. Besides the ball they were playing with, there was now a jumble of blocks near the couch and a ragged-looking cloth doll discarded on the floor. Valentina clanked in the kitchen as she put plates in the cabinet, and for the first time ever, Jesse's apartment felt like a home. Before he did or said something stupid, he headed for the door.

"I'll be at work until about six tonight. You can come down if you need anything, but I don't expect you to start working right away. Take a day or two to settle in, get Katy better. There's canned soup in the sacks I brought up and there's sandwich stuff in the fridge. I usually eat lunch at my desk so you won't see me until dinner."

"I could cook for us," Valentina offered. "I'm not a gourmet chef or anything, but I haven't poisoned anyone yet."

"There's a bag of frozen chicken breasts in the freezer and some canned vegetables in the cabinet. I'll squeeze in a trip to the store during lunch today and restock the groceries. If there's anything in particular you need, just make a list and bring it down."

"We don't really need --"

He cut her off. "Valentina, I've never fed kids before. Make a list of things they like to eat or drink. There's some apple juice in the sacks I brought up. I think the milk in the fridge is still good. If it's not, come get the one from the shop. You don't have to do everything on your own. Let me help you."

She nodded and looked like she might cry. The last thing he wanted to deal with was waterworks so he made a hasty retreat and hurried downstairs. As he entered the shop, the sight of the little family making themselves at home in his apartment wouldn't leave him. He'd never lived with a woman before, not even as a roommate, and the fact he'd liked seeing them in his space scared the shit out of him. It was almost like they were supposed to be there.

Shaking his thoughts away, he went out to greet his employees and get his day started. Maybe if he took an engine apart, he could stop thinking about Valentina's soft blue eyes and silky hair. But no matter how attractive Valentina was, she was off-limits. She was dealing with enough without him lusting after her, even if he had noticed that she had curves in all the right places.

Damn. *You are so screwed.*

Chapter Three

Valentina barricaded Katy in the bed with pillows so she wouldn't roll off. Her sweet baby girl had played for a while after breakfast, and then she'd started coughing and her nose had started running. It felt like her fever had spiked, but Valentina didn't have children's Tylenol, or any kind of fever reducer. She hoped something would come with the pharmacy delivery that still hadn't arrived. It was nearing lunchtime, which meant it was about time to feed Max and then put him down for a nap. She'd noticed a hamper full of clothes in the laundry nook and planned to tackle that while the kids slept. She figured if she was living here rent free, the least she could do was make Jesse's life a little easier. A little laundry and housework wasn't going to kill her.

She'd already washed the dishes and wiped down the kitchen. She'd discovered a vacuum cleaner in the hall closet and thought she'd clean the floors later. Jesse didn't have a lot of cleaning supplies. She'd have loved some furniture polish, floor cleanser for the tiled kitchen and bathroom, and some sort of antibacterial cleaner for the other surfaces around the apartment. A can of Lysol wouldn't hurt either since Katy was spreading germs everywhere.

Jesse had told her to make a list of anything she needed, so she put the cleaning items on her list, along with a package of sponges, and then tried to figure out a menu for the next several days. She felt guilty, asking him to spend so much money. He was already doing so much for them. After she fed Max and put him down for a nap, she quickly crept downstairs with her list in hand. The bay doors were open and she saw Jesse leaning under the hood of a car. She might be a mom, but she was a woman first, and couldn't help but stop and admire the way his jeans hugged his ass.

She entered the garage area and walked straight over to Jesse, ignoring the stares from the other two mechanics. Jesse's hands were covered in grease as he tightened something under the hood. Valentina knew nothing about cars and couldn't have told which part was which. She hated to admit that she didn't even know how to check her oil. Watching Jesse work on the car with such confidence was kind of a turn-on. She'd never really watched a man work with his hands before, but she could see the appeal.

"Jesse," she said softly.

He glanced her way and smiled. Pulling back from the car, he wiped his hands on a rag nearby. "Kids sleeping?"

She nodded. "I brought the list you asked for. If anything on there is too much, we don't have to have it right now. I put some cleaning supplies on there. I noticed you didn't have much up there."

He took the list and scanned over it. "This is all you need?"

"I should be able to make us breakfast, lunch, and dinner for a few days if you get those items."

"What about the kids? Is Katy potty-trained yet?"

"She wears pull-ups, but I can get those later. I still have some."

Jesse searched for a pen and added them to the list. Valentina told him what size and kind she bought.

"What about snacks they like?" he asked.

"Jesse, we don't need --"

He arched an eyebrow, as if daring her to finish her sentence.

Valentina sighed. "Bananas, applesauce, and

goldfish."

Jesse added them to the list. "As soon as I finish with this car, I'll head out and grab what we need. You should rest while the kids nap. Stretch out on the couch and watch a movie or something."

"I've never been one to lie around doing nothing."

He moved a little closer. "Valentina, you're pregnant and stressed out. Stop pushing yourself so hard when you don't have to."

"All right. I'll rest for a while."

"The pharmacy called and said they'd deliver the prescription around two o'clock. They were out of the cough syrup and had to get some from another pharmacy to fill the order. I told them to take it up to the apartment so don't freak out if someone knocks on the door. It's already paid for so all you have to do is sign for it."

Jesse reached out and smoothed his knuckles down her cheek and she leaned into his touch. She couldn't remember the last time someone had touched her so gently. It made her want things she couldn't have. The happily-ever-after she'd always dreamed about seemed even farther away now than ever before. Who would want a pregnant woman with two kids in tow? Jesse was just being nice and she needed to remind herself of that a hundred times a day so she didn't do something stupid.

Maybe she was more tired than she thought because suddenly all she could think about was kissing their rescuer, and she was pretty sure that would be crossing a line. The last thing she wanted to do was jeopardize her kids' future, and Jesse controlled her job and her home for the time being. It would be foolish to risk losing either or both of those things just because her hormones were all over the place.

"I should get back upstairs," she said. "I don't want the kids to wake up and not be able to find me."

He nodded and she forced herself to walk away, but she was almost certain she could feel his eyes on her. It was tempting to look back, but Valentina refused to give in. She walked back up to the apartment and wondered if she'd imagined what she'd felt while standing in his garage. Was there a pull between them, or was it just her? And if there was something there, what was she going to do about it?

Her babies were still asleep when she entered the apartment, both sleeping soundly. Valentina loaded the washing machine and then collapsed on the couch. She had always fallen for guys quickly, and paid the price later. If she were smart, she'd keep as much distance between her and Jesse as she could, and move out at the first opportunity. Besides, just because she noticed he had a fine ass and kiss-worthy lips didn't mean he felt anything for her. He probably just saw her as some pathetic loser who needed rescuing.

While the kids napped, Valentina alternated between watching TV and doing laundry. After she finished washing and drying Jesse's clothes, she folded everything and carried them to his room. The smart thing to do would be to leave them on the bed and let him put them away. Valentina had never claimed to be smart when it came to men. She opened his dresser drawers, locating the correct spot for shirts, jeans, socks, and underwear. Her cheeks warmed a little as she tucked his boxer briefs into a drawer. It didn't escape her notice that her hands were practically caressing the garments that touched his most intimate parts.

Maybe she'd been without sex for too damn long.

Gage hadn't touched her in weeks, which probably should have been her first clue something was wrong. Not that they went at it like rabbits or anything, but he'd always wanted sex at least once a week. For the last three weeks though, he hadn't seemed interested, claiming to be too tired. Now she wondered if he was putting distance between them, preparing to take off and leave her. He had to have known an eviction was coming and yet he'd said nothing to her. She'd been so stupid to trust him.

As usual, she'd seen a pretty face and a great set of abs, and she'd nearly tripped over herself in an effort to gain his attention. And here she was, about to make the same mistake again. At least this time the guy she wanted to kiss was gainfully employed, seemed genuinely kind, and had put her kids first. No one had ever done that before, and she knew that was part of what attracted her to Jesse. It was a stupid infatuation because he'd been so nice to her, and she was an idiot if she tried to make more out of the situation.

There was a knock on the door that pulled her from her thoughts. When she opened it, a young guy who looked like he should still be in high school was holding a bag from the pharmacy and a small clipboard.

"Miss Cupid?" he asked. "I have a delivery for you."

Valentina signed the slip.

"The pharmacist said he added a thermometer and some Motrin to the order. If you need anything else, just call the number on the receipt and we'll bring it right over."

"Thank you," Valentina said with a smile.

She took the bag from him and the boy blushed

as their fingers touched. He stammered a goodbye and took off down the steps. Valentina shut the door and shook her head, thinking he must be shy around women. She carried the bag into the kitchen and read the instructions on the prescription. It didn't need to be refrigerated so she left it on the counter. As soon as Katy woke up, she'd give her the first dose. There was a dropper in the bag too.

She left the Motrin and thermometer on the counter and went to check on the kids again. Both were still sleeping hard and she felt bad. If they hadn't been living in the car the last few days and driven halfway across the country, maybe her babies wouldn't be so worn out. With Katy being sick, she would probably sleep more than usual, but it was unlike Max to take such a long nap. She moved closer to the bed and ran her fingers through his hair, frowning when she felt the heat coming off him. Placing the back of her hand against his forehead, she gasped at how hot he was.

No. Not both kids!

She rushed downstairs, hoping Jesse was still around. As much as she hated to cost him more money, they needed the doctor again. She didn't dare give Max some of Katy's medicine for fear her daughter would need it all. And what if he had something different?

Tears pricked her eyes as she practically ran into the garage. The car Jesse had been working on had the hood shut and he was nowhere in sight. One of the other mechanics came over, scanning her from head to toe. "Do you need something?" he asked.

"I need Jesse."

"He stepped out for a while. Said he had errands to run."

Of course. He was buying the groceries.

"You living with Jesse?" the man asked.

"Um, yes. We just moved in."

"Want me to call his cell and ask him to come back?"

"No. I just… I need Doctor Johnson to come back. He saw my daughter this morning but now my son is sick too."

"Doc will be over at the clinic on Main. They take walk-ins."

But going to the clinic meant waking up her children and trying to get two sick kids down there by herself. There was no way she could carry both of them, and she doubted Max would be up for walking. Tears of frustration welled in her eyes and she blinked them away. If she had a stroller, then she could have managed it, but the one she'd had had broken and there hadn't been time or money to get a new one.

"Are you all right?" the mechanic asked.

"I'll be fine. It's just been a rough day."

"Let me call Jesse."

"No," Valentina said. "He's busy. I don't want to bother him."

"Pretty sure he'd want to know you're about to cry."

Her cheeks burned. "I'll be fine. I'm sorry to have bothered you."

Making a hasty retreat, she went back up to the apartment and tried to think of the best way to get the kids to the clinic. Even if she made it there, how was she going to pay for the visit? Jesse had said the doctor owed him a favor this morning, but a second visit was sure to cost money. Why did one bad thing after another happen to her? She had gotten pregnant a third time -- she loved her baby but it had been unexpected -- then Gage ran out, they were facing eviction, had lived in the car for days, then Katy got sick, and now Max was sick. She was out of money and the weight on her shoulders just got heavier and heavier. Jesse had already done so much for them, but she couldn't ask him for yet another thing. He was going to wonder what sort of train wreck he'd invited into his home.

Valentina sat at the kitchen table and put her head on her folded arms. Sometimes in life you just needed a good cry, and if anyone needed a good cry right now, it was her. Her tears soaked the sleeves of her shirt. When the apartment door slammed a few minutes later, she jumped. Jesse was by her side in a second, his hand on her back as he knelt beside her.

"What's wrong?" he asked. "Did something happen with the kids?"

"Max is sick," she said.

"Come on. We'll take the kids to the clinic. I'll tell my guys I'm taking the rest of the day off. I'll just have to run down later to close up for the night."

"Jesse…"

"Hush. Not one word about how I shouldn't do something."

She sniffled and nodded.

"Get their stuff together and I'll be right back."

While he got things squared away with his shop downstairs, she made sure the diaper bag had everything she might need. Jesse came back a few minutes later and picked up Max, cradling him against his broad shoulder. Valentina lifted Katy and held her close. Downstairs, a large black truck was idling in the parking lot.

"Your car was unlocked so I moved their seats over to my truck," he said as he tucked Max into his car seat. "You must have forgotten to lock it the last time you were down there."

Valentina buckled Katy and then slid into the front passenger seat. The heat was blasting so the inside was toasty warm despite the chill in the air outside. Jesse was not only a lifesaver, he was thoughtful too. The way he took care of them… it was sweet and Valentina felt selfish for wishing it could last forever. She'd always dreamed of a man like Jesse, but had never met one until now. Oh, she'd thought all those frogs she'd dated were princes, but they were all rotten assholes. It figured that when she finally did meet someone really great her life would be a complete wreck.

At the clinic, Jesse carried Max inside while Valentina got Katy. The woman at the front counter in pink scrubs smiled widely when she saw Jesse, and Valentina felt a twinge of jealousy.

"Morning, Jesse," the woman said. "I guess I can see now why you never took me up on my offer."

"Her offer?" Valentina asked before she could stop herself.

Jesse's cheeks flushed and she thought it was kind of cute.

"I asked Jesse out last week. If I'd known he had a girlfriend and two kids moving in with him, I never would have tried poaching."

"Oh, we're --"

Jesse reached over and squeezed her hand, cutting off what she was about to say. Did he want the woman to think they were an item? Valentina couldn't imagine why he wouldn't want to date her. She seemed nice and looked well put together.

"Does Doc Johnson have any openings, Becca?" he asked. "He treated Katy this morning, but now Max is running a fever too."

"I have some forms I'll need you to fill out, but we're not very busy this afternoon so it shouldn't be a problem to work you in. I have to admit, Jesse, you look pretty good with a kid in your arms." A wistful expression crossed the blonde's face.

Jesse accepted the forms and a pen, then ushered Valentina over to some empty chairs. He handed her the documents and took Katy, letting her rest on his other shoulder. The blonde wasn't wrong. He really did look sexy holding her kids with those big, strong arms of his. When the forms were completed and taken back to the receptionist, Valentina took Katy back and prepared herself to wait for however long it took to see the doctor.

Katy woke before they were called back and got a little fussy, but Valentina gave her a cup of juice to keep her quiet. Max continued to sleep while Jesse held him, rubbing a hand up and down her son's back. By the time they were called back, Valentina's arms were hurting from holding Katy so long. In the exam room, she settled in a chair with Katy while Jesse laid Max on the table. Her son stirred and looked around in confusion.

"We're at the doctor, baby," Valentina told him.

He leaned against Jesse and clutched the man's shirt, as if he were afraid to let go. Valentina could relate. She wouldn't mind grabbing hold of Jesse and never letting go either.

Doc Johnson came in and examined her son. "He has a bad cold and fever like Katy. I'll prescribe the same medication for him. If either of them get worse, give me a call and I'll arrange to stop by and see them. I know it's rough getting out with two little ones when they're both sick."

"Thank you," Valentina said. She wanted to ask

about payment, but Jesse beat her to it.

"If you'll send me a bill, Doc, I'll see that it's paid. Valentina and the kids aren't on the company insurance yet."

"I tell you what. My car has been making a clanking noise the last few days. You take a peek at it and we'll call it even on any bills for these two today, and any follow-up visits they may need."

Jesse shook his hand. "Deal."

"I'll call the pharmacy with the prescription. Are you picking it up or do you want it delivered?" Doc asked.

"Delivered, please," Valentina said. "I just want to get my babies home and tucked back into bed."

"That sounds like an excellent plan," Doc said. "I'm only a phone call away if you need anything."

Jesse carried Max back out to the truck with Valentina and Katy trailing after him. He drove them straight back to the apartment. When Valentina approached the apartment steps, she froze and stared in shock. A perfectly good wooden crib and toddler bed were waiting for them, a mattress for each sitting on the steps.

"Jesse, where did those come from?" she asked.

"Mr. Wilson. His wife runs the local library. They're ours to use for however long we need them. I was going to pick up some bedding for them while I was out today, but I never made it to the baby store or the grocery."

Valentina couldn't help but cry again.

"What's wrong?" Jesse asked. "You don't like them?"

"No, they're perfect! Katy's never had a bed before. There was an old rickety playpen she slept in, and Max slept on the pullout couch. No one has ever thought to give my babies beds of their own before."

"Come on," he said softly, reaching down to move the mattresses so they could use the stairs. "Let's put the kids on the bed while I haul this stuff upstairs. I'll run to the store and get bedding for them so they can sleep in their beds tonight."

"You don't have to go buy new stuff. If there's a thrift store in town, they usually sell things like baby and toddler bedding. All they need is a fitted sheet and a blanket. I'd have to wash the new stuff anyway, so there's no point in spending extra money on it."

"Valentina, I'm going to the baby store and that's final."

She nodded and tried to get the kids settled in the bed again while he hauled up the crib and toddler bed. Jesse gave her a long look before he left to run his errands. She didn't know what he thought of her, but that look had shaken her to her core. It wasn't the look of a man just doing a good deed. That look said he wanted them here, and he just might not let them go.

You're crazy, Valentina. You just met the man.

But she remembered something her grandmother had once told her. That when she met the right man, she would know it. Her grandmother had known her grandfather all of three days before they eloped, and they had enjoyed sixty years of marriage before her grandfather passed away.

You are so screwed.

Chapter Four

Jesse ran a hand through his hair as he stared at all the bedding options in front of him. He picked up a set that said it was for a toddler bed and examined the package. Fitted sheet, blanket, and pillowcase. They were white with red and blue trains on them. Boys liked trains, but did Max? Had he ever had a train before? He tossed the set into the basket and moved down to the girly baby bedding. Choosing a pale pink and purple butterfly pattern, he added it to his cart.

He remembered what Mrs. Wilson had said about outlet covers and found the safety area. He tossed in two packages of the outlet covers and some cabinet locks, and picked up a baby gate since one hadn't been delivered with the beds. He hadn't seen more than just the two sippy cups in all of their belongings so he stopped on that aisle and picked up a few more.

As Jesse meandered through the store, he added things to his cart that he thought the kids might want or need, until it was overflowing. His wallet was going to scream after this trip, but it would be worth it to know those babies were taken care of. Valentina had done what she could, and he thought she was a pretty good mom, but those kids weren't going to do without while he was around. He couldn't think of anything more worthwhile to spend his money on.

Jesse loaded the packages into the backseat of his truck and went to the grocery store. He got everything on Valentina's list, and on his way to the checkout, he stopped to admire the flower displays. He'd done everything he could to make the kids comfortable, but he hadn't bought her anything. Not that she'd asked for anything. It had probably hurt her pride to even ask for stuff for the kids, and if he hadn't pushed her, he doubted she'd have said a word about what they needed.

He selected a colorful bouquet and placed it in the cart with a plain vase. Women liked flowers, from what he remembered. He'd never actually given any to someone before, but a few of his foster moms had received them. They'd always smiled and it had seemed to brighten their day. That's what he wanted to do for Valentina. Hell, that was part of what he wanted to do for her. He'd been so damn close to kissing her in the garage earlier, even though he knew it would be a mistake. Not because he didn't want to kiss her, because he really did, but he was trying to gain her trust.

Jesse paid for his purchases and loaded them into the truck then drove back to the apartment. He made several trips up the stairs until all the bags were waiting outside the apartment door on the small deck, then he let himself in and began hauling everything into the apartment. Valentina came down the hall, looking worn out. He could only imagine the strain she had been under today.

She stared at everything with wide eyes. "What is all that?"

"I may have gone a little overboard at the baby store. The rest is groceries." He handed her the flowers and vase. "And these are for you."

She sniffed at the flowers. "No one's ever given me flowers before."

"I thought you could use a little cheering up."

Valentina came closer and leaned up to brush her lips against his cheek, but he turned his head at the last minute. Their lips touched and held. Jesse slowly reached up and wove his fingers through her hair, holding her as his lips moved across hers. Valentina leaned into him and Jesse deepened the kiss. Their tongues tangled and their breath mingled, and Jesse knew in that moment that was in trouble, because no one had ever kissed him as sweetly as Valentina. His blood heated as her curves pressed against him and he fought the urge to haul her straight to his bed.

She pulled away a little, her eyes dark and passion-glazed. "Jesse, I… I think I may be in trouble."

"You're not the only one."

He took the flowers from her and set them on the table before pulling her into his arms. "Where are the kids?"

"Napping."

His mouth slanted over hers again, tasting and teasing. He nipped and licked her lower lip before delving inside. His hands slid down her back and cupped her ass, giving it a squeeze. Damn but the woman was perfect. He lifted her onto the counter, his body spreading her thighs. His mouth dominated hers as his hands slipped under her shirt, caressing the soft skin along her back. His cock throbbed behind his zipper and he ached to be inside of her. No one had ever made him feel so crazy, so out of control.

The groceries lay forgotten as he pulled her shirt over her head and dropped it on the floor. The lace cups of her bra molded to her breasts. He could see the pink of her areolas through the material and he groaned before kissing her again. His hands made quick work of the clasp on her bra and pulled it down her arms. Jesse pulled away only long enough to latch onto one of her pretty nipples, sucking on it hard enough to bring it to a point.

Valentina cried out and pressed a hand to his head, holding him to her. Jesse lavished attention on her breasts until she was panting and begging him for more. He unfastened her jeans and tugged them down her hips. Spreading her legs wide, he admired her pussy, the hair neatly trimmed and her folds glistening with desire. Jesse fell to his knees and buried his head between her thighs.

His tongue swiped against the lips of her pussy. Using his fingers, he spread her wide and feasted on her tender flesh, his lips closing around her clit. Valentina thrust against his face, silently begging for more. Jesse used his lips and tongue to drive her crazy, sending her need higher and higher. Her hips bucked as she neared her release and he rapidly flicked her clit with his tongue. She cried out his name as she came, her nectar flowing over his tongue. Her body trembled as Jesse continued to lick and tease her. When he was satisfied he'd wrung every bit of pleasure from her body, he rose to his feet.

"No one's ever made me feel like that," she said softly.

"You're beautiful, all flushed from your orgasm. I'll picture you just like this the next time I take my cock in my hand."

Her cheeks flushed at his words.

She reached out and cupped him through his jeans, drawing a groan from him. He wanted her more than anything, and while he might have pleasured her in the kitchen, he wasn't about to fuck her on the counter just because he wanted to get off.

"Let me make you feel good," she said.

"Valentina, you don't have to do that."

She licked her lips. "I want to. I want to taste you, the way you tasted me. I want you to come in my mouth."

Jesus. She was trying to kill him.

Valentina slipped off the counter and went to her knees in front of him. Unfastening his pants, she reached in and pulled out his cock. He'd never been harder in his life, and as she stroked his shaft, pre-cum leaked from the tip. Her tongue flicked out and licked it off. It was the hottest thing he'd ever seen. Jesse reached for her, grabbing a handful of her hair.

"Open, sweetheart."

Her jaw dropped and she accepted his cock as he slid it between her lips. Christ, but she felt good. Her tongue curled around his shaft as he slid deeper. He didn't stop until his balls brushed her chin, and then she fucking swallowed on him and he saw stars. Jesse pulled back then pushed forward again, fucking her mouth in long, slow strokes. She clutched his hips as he used her mouth to seek his pleasure. The way her bright eyes stared up at him was an even bigger turn-on.

Jesse stroked faster, her hot mouth welcoming every inch of his cock. Thrusting harder, he felt his balls draw up and a moment later he was shooting cum down her throat. She swallowed every drop and continued to suck on his cock even after his balls had been drained dry. Reluctantly, he pulled out of her mouth and helped her to her feet.

"You are fucking incredible," he said, slamming his mouth on hers for another kiss that left both of them breathless.

His hand skimmed down her soft belly and teased her pussy, finding her slick again. It seemed he wasn't the only one turned on from him fucking her mouth. His cock went from semi-hard to a steel post in a matter of seconds, and he wondered just how long those kids would sleep, because he couldn't think of anything he'd like more than getting balls deep inside of her.

Valentina started tugging his shirt over his head and he tossed it aside. Her hands traced over his pecs and down his abdomen. Her lips met his in a hungry kiss as they explored one another's bodies. Jesse was about to strip out of his jeans when the baby began crying down the hall. Valentina pulled away, her eyes closed as she gave a regretful groan.

Jesse cupped her cheek and kissed her softly. "This isn't finished."

Interest sparked in her eyes. "The kids will be up and down all night if they're sick, but we can try again later. If you'd like."

"Oh, I'd very much like."

She smiled and pulled on her clothes before hurrying down the hall to care for her daughter. Jesse blew out a breath, zipped up his pants, and began putting the groceries away. By the time he was finished, Valentina had reappeared, a cranky Katy in her arms. The baby's face was flushed from her fever and his heart ached for the little girl, for both kids. It was hard enough being sick as an adult, but it really sucked when kids got sick. "What do you need?" he asked.

"I need to give her medicine to her and see if she'll drink some juice. She missed lunch so she's probably a little hungry."

"I'll fill her cup while you give her the meds."

Valentina flashed him a grateful smile as she handed the cup to him.

Jesse helped her care for Katy and checked on Max. They curled up together on the couch, with Katy in Valentina's lap, and watched a movie. The little girl fussed off and on until she finally fell back asleep. Jesse reached for her, cradling her in his arms as he carried her back to the bedroom and tucked her in. When he came back, Valentina was washing the new bedding for the crib.

"I didn't want to wash Max's stuff at the same time in case the red bled in the washer. I should be able to get both washed and dried before bedtime though."

He kissed her cheek and curled an arm around her waist.

They worked together the rest of the afternoon, taking turns with the kids, and Jesse even helped with dinner. Valentina looked exhausted by the time both kids were asleep, hopefully for the night, and he knew that no matter how much he wanted her he wasn't ass enough to ask for sex when she clearly needed sleep.

He took her by the hand and led her down the hall to his room.

"I know I said you could have the spare room with the kids, but I was hoping you might want to sleep in here tonight."

"Is that all we're doing? Sleeping?" she asked.

"I'd love nothing more than to be balls deep inside of you, but you're tired, sweetheart. If the kids are going to be up and down like you said, you need to rest while you can. I promise I'm not going to change my mind if you make me wait a day or two. The kids and your health come first."

She sighed and nodded, then began stripping off her clothes. "Can I sleep in one of your shirts?"

Jesse opened a drawer and tossed her one.

Valentina pulled it on and slipped under the covers. Jesse stripped down to his underwear and crawled in next to her. Her soft body curled against him and he couldn't remember a time he'd ever felt so content. If someone had told him a strange woman was going to land on his doorstep and turn him inside out, he'd have never believed them. But in the matter of one day, Valentina and her kids had managed to wrap him around their little fingers.

He was fucking crazy for moving so fast, especially with a pregnant, single mom, but now that he'd had a taste of her, there was no holding him back. He just hoped she didn't come to regret what they'd shared earlier. Nothing would gut him more than watching her walk away. Whatever it took, he was going to hold onto her with both hands.

Fuck.

"You still awake?" he asked.

"Mm-hm."

"There's something I need to tell you."

"Are you secretly married or gay?"

He barked out a laugh. "Um, no. But I heard some whispers while I was out earlier. It seems the town believes the kids are really mine and we've been having a secret love affair all these years. At least, that's one thing spreading around town. The other is that you kept the kids a secret and sprung them on me today. That one's my favorite because how in the hell did we have an affair that produced two kids and I didn't know anything about either of them?"

Chapter Five

Valentina leaned up on her elbow, her eyes wide. "They're saying what?"

"It's okay. I'm flattered they think those two great kids are mine, and that I have what it takes to hold onto a woman like you."

"You're crazy, you know that, right?"

"I've been called worse."

She laid back down, her head against his shoulder. The town was already talking about them? She wondered how they would react when they learned the truth. Her story wasn't near as glamorous as a secret love affair. At least Jesse was being good-natured about it. He could have gotten pissed that people thought he was a dad times two. Times three if they knew she was pregnant.

Jesse wrapped an arm around her and held her close. Her eyes drifted shut, but just as she was starting to fall asleep, she heard Max calling for her. She wanted to cry, she was so tired, but she pulled herself out of Jesse's embrace, got out of bed, and went to check on her son. His face was still flushed and she grabbed the thermometer out of the kitchen. It was one of the expensive ones she'd never been able to afford. She placed it against his forehead and in seconds it gave her a reading of 101.2. "My poor sweet boy. Momma's going to get you some more medicine, all right?"

Max clutched at her and she picked him up to carry him into the kitchen. She set him down on the counter while she reached for the Motrin. The pharmacy had delivered a second dropper with Max's prescription and she'd marked his with an M so she wouldn't confuse them. After dosing him, she rubbed his back and carried him to the living room.

"Not sleepy," he said as he rubbed his eyes.

She smiled, knowing he was a little liar, but she settled on the couch with him and turned on the TV. There wasn't much this time of night that would interest him, but he didn't seem to care much what was playing. A few minutes later, Jesse sank onto the couch next to them, a pair of sweats hanging low on his hips. His bare chest was a definite distraction, but she tried to focus on the TV.

Katy started crying again just as Max got settled.

"I'll get her," Jesse said, rising from the couch.

"She needs more medicine too," Valentina said.

"I'm a big boy and know how to read bottle labels. You just sit there with Max. I've got this."

She smiled a little when he stopped long enough to kiss the top of her head before walking out of the room. Max snuggled against her and played with the ends of her hair. He'd always been fascinated with it and had pulled out handfuls when he'd been a baby.

Her children meant the world to her. She wondered if she'd unconsciously been trying to find them a new daddy with every boyfriend she moved in with. Unfortunately, she'd picked one loser after another. But was she doing the same thing with Jesse? He deserved so much more than a broke, pregnant woman with two kids. It was obvious from the visit to the clinic earlier that he had other options. She wouldn't doubt that several women around town wanted to take him home.

"You're frowning," Jesse said as he settled next to her with Katy in his arms.

"Just thinking."

"Well now, that sounds like trouble. Starting to wonder what you're doing with me? I'm sure you could get a better offer. Men around here will flock to you if they think you're single."

"Aren't I?" she asked.

His gaze focused on her. "Do you want to be?"

She wasn't sure how to answer that. No, she didn't want to be single. And yes, Jesse was a great catch. She just didn't feel worthy of him. Her daughter cuddled against Jesse's chest and sucked on her fist. Katy and Max both seemed perfectly at ease with Jesse. They'd actually taken to him quicker than they had anyone else. While they would talk to anyone, they didn't *go* to just anyone. It had taken Gage weeks of being around the kids before either would let him hold them. And then he'd seemed awkward and like he didn't really enjoy the experience. She'd thought he just needed time to get used to having kids around, but maybe it had been another sign that things were doomed from the beginning.

"Guess your silence is all the answer I need," Jesse said. He stood and set Katy down on the couch. "Maybe it's best if you sleep in your room tonight."

He started to walk out of the room, but she called out to him. "Jesse, wait."

"I'm not trying to push you for more than you want to give, Valentina. If what happened earlier was a mistake, just say so. Maybe we just got caught up in the heat of the moment. You don't have to share my bed to have a roof over your head. I guess that's how your other relationships worked, but I don't play games like that."

"I wasn't trying to hurt you, Jesse. I just…" She glanced down at the kids before looking up at him again. "Can we talk about this after they go back to bed?"

"Of course."

"Stay?" she asked softly.

His fingers drummed against his thigh as he stared at her long and hard. After a moment, he came back to the couch and sat down, lifting Katy into his lap again. It didn't take long for the kids to fall back asleep and they settled them into their beds. Valentina took Jesse's hand and led him into the bedroom. He was stiff as she shut the door, his shoulders tense and his back straight. It was almost as if he were looking through her as he looked down.

She didn't know how to tell him what she was feeling. She'd never been good saying her thoughts and feelings out loud. Perhaps if she'd used words more than actions, she wouldn't have ended up pregnant three times by three different guys. Not that she would ever wish away her children. They were precious to her.

"Do you know why I ran away when I was seventeen?" she asked.

"Unhappy at home?" he asked.

"I had a great childhood with parents who adored me. Then my dad died when I was ten and my mom got remarried. Things were going great, until I got older and my body started changing. When I turned fifteen, my step dad decided he wanted a different kind of relationship with me. It had started with inappropriate touches that he always laughed off as being accidental. That went on for two years. Until I turned seventeen. Then he came to my room one night when my mom was out of town. He pinned me to the bed and started pulling my clothes off."

"Valentina," he said softly. "You don't have to tell me this."

"I want to. You need to understand. I told you about the dads to my three kids, but you shared everything with me, and I didn't do the same."

"What does your past have to do with what happened in the living room?" he asked.

"Everything."

"All right. I'll listen."

"He raped me that night. After he got up and fastened his pants, he told me if I ever told anyone, he'd kill me. I couldn't sleep the rest of the night, crying as I stared at the door, waiting for him to come back. But he didn't. Not that night."

Jesse looked close to tears as he let Valentina get the story out.

"It happened a few more times before I got up the courage to tell my mom what happened. She didn't believe me, said I was lying. Evidently, he'd told her that I'd been coming onto him whenever she wasn't around. The last time he came to my room, I knew I couldn't stay any longer. I watched him walk out of my room and once I heard his bedroom door shut, I stuffed my backpack with whatever clothes would fit and I snuck out of the house.

"I caught the first bus out of town and ran away to L.A. I lived on the streets until Max's dad found me. Promised me a place to live, and all I had to do was share his bed. I'd seen the other girls on the street, most hooked on drugs and turning to prostitution, and I knew I didn't want that to be me. So I accepted his offer. I figured having to sleep with one guy was preferable to getting paid by lots of guys. And you know about the others."

Jesse reached out and pulled her tight against his chest, stroking her hair.

"I didn't answer you right away because I'm not worthy of a good man like you. The night my step dad came to my room, he made me a whore. I was his dirty little secret, and then I gave it up to anyone who would help me. I'm pathetic."

"You're not pathetic, and I never want to hear you call yourself a whore ever again," Jesse said, his voice gravelly from unshed tears. "And I meant what I said. You don't have to sleep with me to have a place to stay."

"I know," she said softly.

"Is that why you..." She heard him swallow hard. "In the kitchen earlier, was that your way of paying for your keep?"

"No." She pulled back and looked up at him. "I wanted you. Not because you offered me a place to stay, but because I'm attracted to you. It's different with you, Jesse, but you deserve so much better than me."

"Valentina, anyone can see how much you love those kids. You've done whatever you felt was necessary to provide for them and keep your family together, and no one can fault you for that. My heart is breaking for everything you've gone through, but those things were done *to* you, not because you wanted it to happen. You are an amazing, beautiful woman. Never doubt that."

"Jesse." She bit her lip. "Make love to me. Men have used me for sex for five years, but not once has anyone ever made love to me."

"Then we should probably rectify that."

"I'm clean, by the way," she said. "When Gage quit having sex with me, I went and got tested just in case he'd been sleeping around. And you can't get me pregnant, so..."

Jesse smiled at her tenderly. "I'm clean too. Are you saying I don't have to use a condom?"

She nodded shyly. "They don't seem to work

with me anyway. I got pregnant with Max and with Katy when a condom was used."

"Guess that means after this one is born we'd better be super careful."

"You want us around that long?" she asked.

"Yeah. I want you around that long." He lowered his head until his lips touched hers. It felt like the world tilted under her feet as he slipped his tongue into her mouth and gripped her tight. Kissing Jesse was better than anything she'd experienced with other guys, and what they'd done earlier had rocked her world. She couldn't wait to see how explosive things would be between them.

Jesse slowly undressed her and then removed his own clothes. Her breasts brushed against him as he backed her toward the bed, and her nipples pebbled from the contact. Jesse eased her back onto the bed and followed her down, his body pressing her into the mattress. She welcomed his weight and parted her thighs so she could wrap her legs around him.

He alternated between kissing her lips and playing with her breasts. His teeth grazed her nipple and sparks shot straight to her clit. Valentina felt his cock rub against her thigh, the head brushing against her pussy. His lips closed around the tip of her breast and he sucked until her toes were curling and her pussy ached for him to fill her.

Jesse's fingers brushed against her slick pussy, the touch light and teasing. "I want another taste of this sweet honey."

She wanted that. So much.

Jesse slipped down the bed and spread her wide. Valentina gripped the bedding as his tongue swiped against her folds. Jesse moaned, the vibration making her clit throb. He speared her with his tongue before licking up to her clit and circling it. His hands gripped her thighs, holding them apart, as his mouth sucked, licked, and tormented her. Valentina trembled as he played with her clit, flicking it with his tongue then sucking it into his mouth.

"Jesse," she said breathlessly, her hand going to his hair. Her fingers wove through the tresses. She wasn't certain if she was just holding on or trying to pull him tighter against her pussy.

His talented lips and tongue drove her to dizzying heights. Jesse shifted and his thumb pressed against her clit, rubbing it in small, tight circles. His tongue licked and tasted her before thrusting deeper. He fucked her with his tongue, stroking it in and out of her tight channel, while he played with her clit. Valentina bit her lip to keep from being too noisy as her climax rushed over her, leaving her shaken and wanting more.

Even after she came, he licked and teased her. He drew her clit into his mouth and sucked on it relentlessly until she came a second time, her thighs clenching on his shoulders. Jesse released her clit, only to softly pet her with his fingers, every stroke against the sensitive bundle of nerves made her twitch and whimper.

"So pretty and pink," he said as he came over her, his cock teasing her folds. "You can still change your mind. We can stop right now and I'll just hold you."

"I want to feel you inside of me."

Jesse reached between their bodies and spread her pussy as his cock slowly sank into her. He stretched her impossibly wide, and didn't stop until he was balls deep inside of her. He ground himself against her, his pelvis stroking her clit, sending another shockwave of pleasure through her. Jesse kissed her tenderly, the tang of her orgasm on his lips. His thrusts were slow and steady, as if he had all the time in the world. Her nails raked his back as her legs closed around his hips.

He gripped her hip with one hand, pulling her tighter against him with every stroke. He thrust deeper, harder. Valentina felt like the world was spinning around her. Being with Jesse was beyond anything she'd ever experienced before. She felt closer to him than anyone else she'd ever been with. Sweat slicked his skin and his eyes burned with an intensity that left her breathless.

"Play with your clit, baby. Make yourself come. I need to feel you squeezing my dick."

Valentina whimpered as his words made her even wetter for him. She reached between them and her fingers brushed over her clit.

Jesse looked down, watching her. He pulled his body away from her and his gaze darkened.

"Fuck, sweetheart. Your pussy looks so damn good wrapped around my cock. You better tease that clit good. Keep rubbing."

Her fingers moved faster and she felt herself getting close.

"Think you can come when I tell you to?" Jesse asked.

"I -- I don't know. I've never tried."

"Keep rubbing that clit, baby, and when I tell you to, I want you to pinch it. You'll come harder than you ever have before. I want to feel this pussy gush all over my cock."

His words heated her from the inside out and her thighs trembled. When he gave the word, she pinched her clit and stars burst behind her eyes. Valentina cried out as her body tensed and wave after wave of pleasure rolled over her. Their bodies slapped together and she felt him coming, a warm splash of cum bathing her inner walls. Jesse didn't stop thrusting and Valentina bowed off the bed as she came again.

When he stilled over her, his cock buried inside her, Valentina knew that he'd just ruined her for other men. No one would ever be able to top what they'd just shared. Jesse kissed her after he'd caught his breath and gazed down at her tenderly.

"Sweetheart, I think you just turned me inside out."

She smiled softy. "Thank you, Jesse. For showing me what it's supposed to be like."

"I can promise you it's never been that good before." He ground against her, his cock still semi-hard. "This is the sweetest pussy I've ever tasted, and the best I've ever had."

Jesse pulled out and rolled to his side. Valentina curled against him and his arm came around her, pulling her closer. Her heart was pounding in her chest, but she'd never felt better.

"You give me a few minutes to catch my breath, and we'll see if we can't do better," he said.

Better? Holy hell. If he did any better, she wouldn't be able to walk ever again.

Chapter Six

Jesse yawned and stared at the computer screen through blurry eyes. He'd already downed two cups of coffee and still had the energy of a slug. Between the kids getting up and down all night, and burning up the sheets with Valentina every chance he had last night, he was damn exhausted, but in the best of ways. He couldn't think of a better reason to be so wiped out.

He'd left Valentina asleep in his bed, and both kids snoring in their room. It had been hard dragging himself out of bed this morning. Valentina had been snuggled against his chest, and he would have loved getting to spend a day in bed with her. Having to be quiet in the morning while he got ready had been a little strange, but he liked having a family under his roof. They'd only shared one night together, but Jesse was hoping there would be many more.

It was nearing nine in the morning and he still hadn't heard any noise from upstairs. He knew Valentina had to be worn out from the stress of both kids being sick and then him keeping her up all night. He really should have let her rest, but damn it was hard to keep his hands off her. He promised himself he'd do better tonight. Maybe run her a hot bath and have dinner delivered so she wouldn't feel like she had to cook.

Jesse scrubbed his hands up and down his face a few times and then stood and stretched. From what he'd seen of the orders this morning, it was going to be a light day on the shop floor. Perfect time to get caught up on paperwork, except he couldn't focus on it. Henry and Marco were both working on cars when he stepped out on the floor. The waiting room was empty, so they'd been drop-offs.

Henry glanced his way. "No offense, boss, but you look like hell."

Jesse smiled a little. "Yeah. Long night."

"It's rough when both kids are sick," Henry said. "It always happens that way at my house. If Rachel comes down with something, it's not long before Emily has it too."

"Thankfully, Max and Katy just have a cold, but they were up and down all night. Neither one have figured out how to blow their noses, so Valentina was having to use one of those bulb things by this morning. Both kids woke up coughing and stopped up around three o'clock."

"Why don't you take the day off?" Henry suggested. "Marco and I can handle the orders for today. You haven't had a day off in a long while."

"The only job on the books tomorrow is Mr. Paulson's Honda. The new transmission came in this morning. I say you take tomorrow off too," Marco said. "We're closed Sunday. You could have a three-day weekend to spend with your family."

Was there anyone in town who didn't think Valentina's kids were his?

"Boss, we've got it handled," Henry said. "And if an emergency crops up, we can call your cell. If your woman is worn out from caring for the kids, you should be there to help her."

It was really hard to argue with them, when he wanted to take a day off. He rubbed the back of his neck and nodded. "All right. I'll take off until Monday, but call the second you need anything."

Jesse left his computer up in his office in case they needed to access any of the files, double-checked the schedule, and then headed upstairs. When he let himself into the apartment, it was too damn quiet. If he hadn't seen Valentina's car in the parking lot, he might have thought she'd left. Jesse locked the door and went to check on the kids. Both were sleeping hard, but they were both having to breathe through their mouths. Poor babies.

He watched them sleep for a minute before checking on Valentina. She'd burrowed under the blankets until he could only see the top of her head. He frowned when he realized there was a chill in the air. Jesse kicked off his boots and went to check the thermostat. Sixty-seven. What the hell?

It said the heat should be on, but he walked to the living room and held his hand up to a vent. Chilly air poured out of it. There was no way he could have a busted heater with two sick kids in the house. Jesse pulled his phone from his pocket and called Don's Heating and Air.

"Hey, Jesse," Don said after picking up.

"Don, how busy are you today?"

"I'm watching ESPN and eating pretzels. Does that tell you anything?"

"Can you come take a look at the heater in the apartment? It's blowing cold air and I've got two sick kids."

"Damn. So it's true?" Don asked. "You really moved a woman and two kids into your place? It's all anyone's been able to talk about since yesterday morning."

Small town living at its finest. "Yeah, it's true. They're all asleep, but the apartment is getting cold."

"I'll be there in fifteen minutes."

"Thanks, man. I owe you."

Don snorted. "You never did let me pay for that engine rebuild last year. Let's just call it even."

Jesse hated that Don felt like he owed him. Don's

business had taken a huge hit last year when he'd had to close up shop for four weeks while his wife was treated in Dallas for some rare medical condition. When the engine had gone out in Don's truck, he'd seen the look on Don's face when he'd seen the bill. Jesse had told him not to worry about it and ripped it up. As much as he was in business to make money, he wasn't without a heart.

"That will be fine, Don," Jesse said. "But if the repairs cost more than what you owed on your car, I expect you to let me pay the balance."

"All right, Jesse. I'll see you soon."

He disconnected the call and went to check on the kids again. Both were huddled under their blankets, and still felt a little warm to the touch. He'd watched Valentina use the thermometer and knew how it worked now. He grabbed it out of the dresser and checked both kids, relieved that Katy's temp was almost normal and Max's had dropped under one hundred. It seemed the meds were already starting to work. But if he didn't get the apartment warmed up soon, he worried they could get sicker.

He kept watch for Don and let him in before he could even knock.

"Do you know if there's a separate system for the apartment or is the heat out downstairs too?" Don asked.

"Just up here so I think it's a separate unit."

"I'll take a look and see what's up with it."

Jesse gave him some space and brewed a pot of coffee while he waited. He poured himself a cup and leaned against the counter. When Don came to the kitchen a little while later, he had a grim expression.

"Your heat exchanger is cracked. I can replace it for about fifteen hundred, but your unit is pretty damn old. Even if I fix it now, you may need to replace the unit next year."

"How much is a new one versus the cost of repairing this one?" Jesse asked.

"Like I said, fifteen hundred to fix this one. For a new one? Assuming you want the cheapest furnace I can get, with labor added in, you're looking around four or five thousand. I can't give you an exact amount until I locate a furnace."

Jesse whistled.

"I'd deduct the two thousand I owe you for the truck. So you'd only have to pay two or three thousand, or I can repair it at no cost to you," Don said. "It's the least I can do."

"If you replace it, can you get a new one installed today?"

"It's early enough I might be able to pull it off. Depends on how far I have to drive to get the new furnace. Might be tomorrow. Do you have some space heaters you could use in the meantime?"

"No," Jesse said. "But I can go get some."

"Cole's Hardware had some on clearance when I was in there yesterday. I think they were marked down to fifteen dollars. Wouldn't hurt to grab a few. Even if I can replace the unit today, you'll be without heat for hours."

"Thanks, Don. See what you can do on the furnace and let me know if you're coming back today or tomorrow."

Don nodded and let himself out.

Jesse finished his coffee and went to wake Valentina. Even though she needed her sleep, he figured she'd want to know the heat was out so she could keep an eye on the kids. She was still burrowed under the blankets when he stepped into the room, and he slowly peeled back the layers until he found her.

Valentina stretched and opened her eyes. "Morning."

"Good morning, beautiful. I have some bad news."

She bolted upright. "Katy? Max?"

"They're fine, but the heat is out. I have someone looking for a new furnace, but we could be without heat until tomorrow sometime. I'm going to run over to the hardware store and pick up some space heaters to warm the bedrooms and the living room. We should probably keep the kids bundled as much as possible."

"I should make breakfast in case they wake up hungry," she said.

"Dress warm. It's not freezing in here yet, but the temperature is dropping. I'll get back with the heaters as quick as I can. If the kids take a bath later, we'll use our bedroom heater to warm the bathroom."

"Our room?" she asked, smiling softly.

"I was hoping you'd want to share it with me. I can make some room for your clothes today if you want to unpack them. We could take out the bed that's in the kids' room to give them more space."

Valentina bit her lip. "It sounds like you plan for us to be here a while."

"I'm moving too fast again, aren't I?"

"A little. But I like it."

"Why don't you stay warm in bed while I get those heaters, and when I get back, if the kids are still asleep, I'll start the shower for you?"

"Are you saying I smell?"

He grinned. "Actually, I was hoping you'd let me scrub your back."

"It's probably a good thing I'm already pregnant, or you'd have me knocked up in no time. I swear you're insatiable."

"Only with you." He kissed her softly. "I'll be back soon."

Valentina slipped her hand under his shirt to caress his abs. "Better make it real soon. The kids could wake up any minute."

"Then I'll break every speed limit in town."

Jesse smiled, kissed her once more, and hurried down to his truck. The sooner he got back, the sooner the apartment could warm up, and the sooner he could get his hands on the sexy woman in his bed. The last time he'd felt this damn horny had been after his two years in juvie. Longest damn time he'd gone without sex and he'd more than made up for it, screwing every woman in sight for the next six months.

But fuck if he didn't want Valentina more than he'd wanted to sink into that first pussy after being freed. And it wasn't just because she was so damn sexy, or how well they fit together. The more he learned about her, the more he admired her and liked her. If anyone could make him think longer term than a few dates, it was Valentina.

* * *

Jesse hadn't been gone five minutes before both kids woke up. They weren't as fussy as the previous day, but she could tell they still didn't feel well. She suctioned out their noses so they could breathe easier, changed Katy's pull-up, and helped Max in the bathroom. She tucked them both back into bed while she made breakfast. She was plating the eggs and bacon when Jesse made it back home, carrying three space heaters.

He set up the one in the kids' room first, then placed the other two in the other rooms. Valentina had just put the plates on the table when Jesse came in carrying a kid in each arm. It had been a while since she'd sat down to a family breakfast. With Gage, she'd always fed him first and then the kids, only because he'd demanded it be done that way. She hadn't been allowed to fix her plate until everyone was done, and if Gage asked for seconds, that didn't always leave very much.

Jesse eyed the two pieces of bacon on her plate and the mountain she'd placed on his. He took two off his plate and set them down on hers, then winked at her. Her cheeks warmed, and she focused on the kids, helping them eat. Max had gotten pretty good at feeding himself, but still made a mess, and Katy got more on her cheeks and chin than in her mouth.

"After we eat, why don't I spread a blanket on the floor in the living room for the kids? We can put a cartoon on for them," Jesse said.

"Won't the floor be the coldest place for them?" she asked.

"We'll blow the space heater across the blanket, make it nice and warm for them. We might be a little chilly on the couch, but I figured we could huddle together under a blanket."

The look in his eyes said he had more than that planned and she fought a smile.

"I know we're not officially together or anything," Jesse said, "but you're living here, and we're sleeping together. Tomorrow is Valentine's Day. I thought maybe we could do something special."

Valentina grimaced. "I hate that damn holiday."

"Why?"

"Hello! My name is Valentina Cupid. Do you know much I was teased every Valentine's Day?"

"I promise the only teasing I'll do will be the kind you like."

Her cheeks flushed.

"I know the kids are sick, and you haven't met anyone around here you'd probably trust to babysit, so I thought we could just do something here after they go to bed tomorrow night."

"You don't have to do anything for me, Jesse. You've done enough for us already."

He reached over and took her hand. "I haven't done anything I didn't want to do. When's the last time you let someone do something special for you?"

"Um, never? The guys I've dated weren't exactly romantic. Their idea of a perfect Valentine's Day was…" She glanced at the kids and lowered her voice. "As many blowjobs as they wanted that day."

"Assholes."

She wasn't going to argue with that.

Jesse leaned in closer. "How about this? We spend the day doing crafts with the kids and watching whatever movies they select, I have a family dinner delivered, then after the kids are in bed, I pamper you."

"You want to do crafts with the kids?" she asked skeptically.

"Well, I obviously would need to go get supplies, but sure. It could be fun."

"Jesse, when's the last time you were around a three-year-old who had access to markers and glue?"

"Uh, never."

"Better get washable glue and markers. It wouldn't hurt to buy one of those Mr. Clean magic erasers too. Maybe a two-pack." She pushed her plate away. "And a drop cloth."

"You make it sound like they're going to destroy the apartment."

"It takes about two seconds of a toddler being

unsupervised for you to need new furniture, newly painted walls, new carpet, and spend the rest of the night in the ER to have some object unglued from their hand."

His eyes widened and he looked at the kids then back at her. "Got it. Washable everything."

"And, Jesse?"

He glanced at her.

"I'd love to spend Valentine's night with you, no matter what you have planned."

He grinned and finished his breakfast. After she'd cleaned up the table and gotten the kids situated on the pallet Jesse had made, he took off, claiming to need supplies for tomorrow. Valentina had to admit that she was curious what a "special" night entailed. She'd never had a boyfriend in high school, and the losers who had fathered her kids hadn't been romantic in the least.

Jesse was gone for two hours and when he returned, his arms were full of sacks. He set some on the kitchen table then carried the rest down the hall. Valentina was curious and went to check out the sacks in the kitchen. She found two bottles of washable glue, some washable crayons and markers, two packs of construction paper, safety scissors, and several bottles of glitter. She snickered.

"What's so funny?" Jesse asked as he came down the hall.

"You bought glitter."

"So? I thought the kids might like to make sparkly hearts or something."

"Jesse, unless you want your apartment to sparkle for the rest of your life, it's best if you hide the glitter. That stuff will migrate everywhere, even into your underwear, and it will never come out. You can get some on your clothes and wash them a hundred times and you'll still find sparkles on them."

His eyebrows rose. "All right. So maybe the glitter wasn't the best part of my plan. I'd have to turn in my man card if I wore sparkly underwear."

"So what you're telling me is that if you piss me off the best form of revenge would be glittering your underwear drawer?" She grinned. "Or maybe I should pour the glitter into your shower gel. Then your cock can sparkle too."

"That's cold, woman. A man has his pride. I can't have a sparkling dick."

She shrugged. "I bet the Team Edward fans would like it. I'd just have to glitter the rest of you and then you could be a Cullen. You're pretty enough."

"I have no idea what you just said, but it sounds horrifying."

Valentina smiled and pulled him toward the living room. "Come on, we have some cuddling to do. I found the kids' favorite movie on cable so they'll be entertained until it goes off. With some luck, they may fall asleep watching it."

"You're just anxious to have your back scrubbed."

She leaned in closer, her lips brushing his ear. "I was hoping you'd like to rub some other areas too."

His gaze scanned her bare legs. He'd told her to dress warm, but she'd liked the look in his eyes last night when he'd seen her wearing his shirt and nothing else. Feeling daring, she'd decided not to change just yet. The heated look was back, and she was glad she'd remained in his shirt.

Jesse took her hand and led her over to the couch, pulling her down next to him, and covered them with the blanket he'd tossed on the arm earlier.

Neither kid paid them any attention, both staring at the TV like it was the most fascinating thing ever.

"Why don't you sit in my lap?" he said softly so the kids wouldn't hear.

Valentina glanced at the kids again to make sure they weren't watching, then she settled across Jesse's lap. Jesse wrapped an arm around her waist and lifted the T-shirt with his other hand. Her breath caught when he'd pushed the shirt up to her waist. She could feel the denim of his jeans under her bare ass, and she couldn't remember a time she'd ever been more turned on.

Jesse's eyes smoldered as he nudged her thighs apart and his fingers brushed over her pussy. A tremor racked her body at the promise of more pleasure. Her heart raced and she kept one eye on the kids, wanting to make sure they didn't have a clue what was happening. The blanket shielded her bared body and Jesse's talented fingers, but she'd have to be careful not to make a lot of noise.

He traced lazy circles on the lips of her pussy, teasing her with light caresses. His fingers spread her open and he dipped a digit into her channel, slowly fucking her. She wanted to spread her legs wider, open herself completely. His wet finger pulled out of her and slid up to toy with her clit.

"God, Jesse. That feels so…" She moaned quietly.

His lips caressed her ear. "If we were alone, I'd put your legs on my shoulders and I'd lick your pussy until you were screaming my name." He rubbed her clit harder. "I'd suck this little bud into my mouth and flick it with my tongue until you were clawing at me, begging."

Her breathing grew harsh as his words turned her on even more.

"I'd get you so worked up, tasting every inch of this pretty pussy. You like my mouth on you, don't you?"

"Yes."

"I'd fuck you with my tongue like I did last night, but it still wouldn't be enough would it?"

She bit her lip and shook her head.

"Because what you really want is my cock pounding into this sweet pussy, isn't it?"

"I want that so much."

He traced the shell of her ear with his tongue as he pinched her clit. "One of these days, I'm going to fill every hole with my cum. You're going to suck my cock, long and hard, until I come down your throat. Then I'll take this pussy, make it mine, and fill you with my cum. And when you think you can't take any more, I'm going to flip you over and fuck that tight ass of yours."

Her breath caught in her throat.

"You'll beg me to fuck that ass hard and deep, beg me for my cum."

He pinched her clit a little harder and she came, her pussy soaking his hand. Valentina bit her lip hard to keep from crying out. Jesse continued to stroke and tease her, drawing out her orgasm until she trembled in his arms, and still he played with her.

"You think you get off with just one orgasm?" he asked. "I own those orgasms, baby, and you are nowhere near done yet. You're going to come for me again."

Valentina whimpered. She looked down at her kids and noticed Katy was asleep and Max's eyes were starting to drift shut. Focusing on Jesse again, she spread her legs a little further and let him take her to paradise again.

"How long will they sleep?" he asked.

"I don't know. Maybe a half hour or so?"

"Long enough."

He stood, lifting her into his arms.

"I won't hear them from the bedroom," she said.

"Then we won't go far."

He walked around the couch and eased her down his body. Jesse spread the blanket on the floor and knelt on it, pulling Valentina down. They were out of view of the kids, but would still hear them if they woke up. He pushed the shirt up to her waist again and spread her legs wide before settling between her thighs.

His mouth latched onto her and Valentina nearly saw stars. He gripped her hips, his fingers digging into her ass cheeks, as he held her against his mouth, devouring her, licking and sucking every inch of her pussy. He spread her ass and toyed with her tight hole, making her gasp and jerk. She'd never let anyone play back there before, but the light strokes Jesse was giving her only made her desire escalate.

He tongue-fucked her thoroughly, giving her so much pleasure she nearly couldn't breathe. She came twice before he backed off, and still her body craved more from him.

He stared down at her, tracing the lips of her pussy with his fingertip. "So damn beautiful."

"More," she begged.

He grinned and leaned down to kiss her. "Not yet, baby. Later. I'll give you whatever you want tonight."

"Promise?"

He kissed her again. "Promise. Now go shower and dress in case Don comes back to fix the heat. I'll watch the kids."

She tugged the shirt down and got up. "You told me last night I'd turned you inside out. You do the same thing to me."

Jesse smiled. "Best news I've heard all day."

Valentina pressed her lips to his once more before hurrying down the hall. She didn't know what had made her choose his parking lot the other night, but she would be forever grateful to whatever force had been guiding her. Finding Jesse was the best thing that had ever happened to her.

Chapter Seven

Valentine's Day was one exhausting adventure after another. Jesse had ordered breakfast from the diner and picked it up, then had pizzas delivered for lunch. They'd spent the day doing crafts with the kids and watching movies. Both Max and Katy seemed to be feeling better, at least if the disaster that was his kitchen and living room were any indication. Valentina hadn't been kidding about buying the washable stuff and those special sponges. The kids had gotten marker and glue on the kitchen table, the carpet, and Max had drawn stick figures on the wall, but it looked suspiciously like a Mom, Dad, and two kids. Jesse's throat had tightened with emotion and he'd wondered if it was supposed to be the four of them.

He'd had more fun spending the day with Valentina and the kids than he'd ever had before. If anyone had told him he'd enjoy family life, he'd have laughed. But being with the three of them made him wish they weren't just staying temporarily. Valentina hadn't started working for him yet, but he knew she would soon, and then when she had enough money saved, she and the kids would move out. And Jesse would lose the best thing that had ever happened to him.

Valentina was bathing the kids and getting them into their pajamas while he cooked dinner. It wasn't anything fancy, just chicken alfredo with some Italian bread on the side, but he'd wanted to make their Valentine's dinner himself, even if he wasn't the greatest chef in the world. Even he couldn't screw up chicken, noodles, and sauce from a jar. While the noodles cooked, he used the special sponges to clean the table, then cleaned the glue off the chairs the kids had used.

By the time Valentina came back to the kitchen with both kids in tow, dinner was ready and he'd set the table. Both kids had a sippy cup of milk, and he'd gotten sparkling grape juice for him and Valentina, having learned from a woman at the grocery that pregnant women couldn't drink. Of course, now the town would know she was pregnant and even more rumors would fly.

"Doesn't this look great, guys?" Valentina asked the kids. "What do you say?"

"Thank you, Daddy," Max said.

"Da, Da, Da, Da," Katy babbled.

Valentina gave him a startled look and Jesse felt that tightness in his throat again. He gave her a smile to let her know it didn't bother him that the kids had called him dad. "You're welcome."

"I thought maybe I should start work tomorrow," Valentina said. "The kids are feeling better so there's no reason to stay home all day."

"You want to start a half day and see how it goes?" he asked.

"You'd be okay with that?" Valentina asked.

"Of course. The kids come first, right?"

An emotion crossed her face that he couldn't quite label and then she nodded and went back to eating. As Valentina fed Katy, he helped Max. It was nice sitting around the table like this, and having Valentina and the kids with him filled a hole he hadn't realized was even there. When their meal was finished, he cleaned up the kitchen while Valentina watched a cartoon with the kids. He couldn't help but watch the clock and wonder when he'd get some alone time with her. It had been awesome having a family day, but they'd been so busy with the kids they hadn't had time just for each other.

While Valentina tucked the kids into bed and read them a story, he ran a hot bath and filled the bathroom with the scented candles he'd purchased. If anyone deserved a night to relax and be pampered, it was Valentina. Even though they'd only been together a few days, he'd noticed her life revolved around her kids and she didn't really take time to enjoy anything. Her showers were quick, in case the kids needed her. She ate quickly, so she could take care of the kids. The only time she'd really let loose were the times he'd given her thigh-trembling orgasms, and even then she listened for the kids.

Valentina stepped into the hall just as he was shutting off the water, and he took her by the hand and led her into the bathroom. Her eyes widened when she saw the steaming tub and soft candlelight. Jesse had set his iPhone on the counter and had classical music playing at a low volume to help relax her further.

"You're going to take some time just for you," he said. "I'll listen for the kids, but I don't want you out of that water until it's cooled. You deserve a little time to yourself, then we're going to spend some time together."

"Jesse…" Her eyes misted with tears. "No one's ever done something like this for me before."

"I want to take care of you, Valentina. I know after everything you've been through you're not used to that, but if you'll let me, I'll help you however I can. Whether it's feeding the kids, running a bath for you, or holding you while you sleep. I never knew my life was missing anything until I brought you and the kids here."

"Jesse, what are you saying?" she asked, a tear trickling down her cheek.

"I'm saying even though it's fast, and you really don't know me all that well, I'm hoping you'll consider staying here. Permanently. I don't want the three of you to go in a few months after you've saved up some money. I want you to stay here with me, make this place a home. I know I told you before I planned to be in your life for a long time to come, but I want more than that. I want us to be a family."

She bit her lip as another tear slipped down her cheek.

"Just think about it," he said. "I'll close the door and let you enjoy your bath. Don't worry about the kids for a little while. I've got them."

"Thank you," she said softly.

Jesse shut the door and leaned his forehead against it. He hoped he hadn't said too much too soon, but he wanted her to know how he felt. There had been women in his life, even though none were serious, but he'd never felt anything like he did when he was with Valentina. She made him want to be a better man, a man deserving of the incredible family staying under his roof. When the kids had called him dad tonight, it had been the happiest moment of his life. It should have scared the hell out of him and sent him running for the door, but it just felt right. He wanted to be their dad, wanted to be someone they could look up to.

He wasn't perfect, far from it, but he felt like the four of them were perfect together. And when Valentina had her baby, he wanted to be there with her every step of the way. She'd trusted the wrong men before, but Jesse was determined to be the *right* guy. He wouldn't abandon her, no matter how tough things got. The thought of running out on her and the kids horrified him. They needed stability, all of them, and he wanted to be the one to give it to them.

His reasons weren't completely selfless. Valentina was a gorgeous woman, and they were dynamite in bed, but he liked her for more than what she did to him in the bedroom. She was sweet and caring, and from what he'd seen, she was a great mom. She made him feel this protective urge to guard her and the kids with his life, and he would, gladly.

He heard the tub draining and a moment later, Valentina stepped into the hall wrapped in a towel. His heart pounded as his gaze traced over her lovingly, from the messy bun on top of her head, to the tips of her cute little toes. Valentina came closer and reached for his hand, guiding him to the bedroom. She closed the door softly and reached for the front of her towel, letting it fall to the floor.

Jesse swallowed hard. "You don't have to do this. I can just hold you tonight."

"You've been amazing to me and the kids all day, taking care of our every need. It's time someone took care of your needs," she said. Her hand cupped him. "You can't tell me you don't want me."

"I always want you," he admitted.

Her hand trailed down his chest and his abdomen tightened.

"No one's ever been as gentle with me as you are," she said. "Guys have always taken what they wanted. I'd thought all men were like that, until I met you."

"Not everyone's an asshole," he said.

She smiled a little. "Maybe not, but all of the guys in my life have always been assholes. You learned from your mistakes and you've made something of your life, Jesse. I've never met anyone like you."

"I meant what I said," Jesse said. "I want you and the kids to stay here. I won't lie, I like having you in my bed, but I like… I like feeling like we're a family. When they called me dad tonight…"

She wrapped her arms around his waist and rested her head on his chest. "If you want us to stay, we'll stay. I know I should be stronger and move out like I'd planned, but I like being here with you. I like how you make the kids smile, and you make me feel special. What we have may not last. Like you said, we're moving really fast, but I'm willing to find out if you are."

Jesse tipped her chin up and kissed her softly. "I'd really like that."

She tugged on his shirt. "You've already made this the most awesome Valentine's Day ever, but I was hoping there might be some orgasms in store for the rest of the night."

Jesse laughed and pulled his shirt over his head. "I think I can manage that. How many do you want?"

"As many as you want to give me," she said, pressing her lips to his. "But why don't you let me do something for you first?"

"Valentina." He groaned as she sank to her knees in front of him.

She unfastened his jeans and tugged them and his boxer briefs down his thighs. Jesse stepped out of them, kicking them across the room. Valentina licked her lips as she eyed his cock, as if it were a treat she couldn't wait to taste. Jesse feathered his fingers through her hair, and as her lips closed around his cock, he gripped her hair tight.

His heart pounded and he kept his gaze fastened on Valentina. The sight of her swallowing his dick was nearly enough to make him come. The shaft was slick from her saliva as she licked, sucked, and teased. Valentina reached up and cupped his balls, rolling them in her hand. His knees nearly buckled from the pleasure zinging through him. Her tongue curled around his cock as she pulled back, then took him all the way to the back of her throat, swallowing on him.

"Fuck, Valentina! That feels so damn good."

She pulled back and licked her lips. "I want you to come in my mouth."

Jesse groaned and knew if she kept talking like that, he'd come any minute. Valentina sucked him harder and faster. Jesse felt his balls draw up and then he was coming, filling her mouth. Valentina sucked him dry, swallowing every drop. Even after his explosive orgasm, she continued to lick and tease him, her soft lips making him shudder. She didn't stop until he was hard again and then she led him over to the bed, pushing him down before lying beside him.

"I was supposed to be making tonight special for you, not the other way around," he said.

"You've made all day special for me."

He kissed her, his tongue delving between her lips for a taste. "I want you," he murmured against her lips.

"Then take me."

"I want tonight to be perfect for you," he said.

"Jesse, the way you touch me, the way you make me feel… every time we're together it's perfect."

He kissed her, devouring her mouth as if it were the last kiss they'd ever share. Jesse rolled her under him, settling between her thighs. His lips never left hers as his cock slowly sank into her, her wet heat welcoming him. He groaned as he used slow, deep thrusts that ignited every nerve ending in his body. It was like she was made just for him, the way they fit perfectly together.

Her silken walls tightened on his cock as her

nails bit into his shoulders. She was so slick, so ready for him. He stroked in and out of her with ease, as he drove into her faster, harder. Valentina's legs tightened around him and her body flushed with her impending orgasm. Jesse reached between their bodies, his thumb pressing on her swollen clit. She gasped under him as he circled it slowly.

"Jesse!" she cried out, her body straining against his.

"Come for me, sweetheart."

She whimpered and he rubbed her clit faster, until she shattered under him. Her pussy squeezed him tight, and Jesse gripped her hips, driving into her over and over until he spilled himself inside of her. They panted for breath, staring into one another's eyes.

Katy cried from the other room and Valentina bit her lip. "I'm sorry. It looks like our night is getting interrupted."

"Why don't you stay here? I'll go check on her."

"Are you sure?" she asked.

"I'm positive." He kissed her softly. "Don't go anywhere. I'm not done with you yet tonight."

Valentina grinned as he rolled out of bed and pulled on a pair of sweat pants. Jesse's gaze devoured her before he opened the bedroom door and disappeared down the hall. Katy was standing up in her bed, tears rolling down her cheeks.

"Hey, sweet pea. Did you have a bad dream?" Jesse asked, lifting her out of the bed.

"Da, da, da, da," she babbled.

"Daddy's got you." He cuddled her against his chest and ran a hand up and down her back. She took a shuddering breath and then relaxed against him. Jesse nuzzled her head, smelling her sweet baby scent, and grabbed her blanket out of her bed. He draped it over her and carried her into the living room, where he walked the floor until her breaths evened out.

He looked up and saw Valentina leaning against the wall, his shirt covering everything important and leaving her sexy legs on display.

"You're really good with her," Valentina said. "I think she loves you already."

"I love her too," Jesse said, his heart feeling full as he held Katy and looked at the woman who was fast claiming his heart.

"Why don't you put her back to bed? I think she'll sleep a while now," Valentina said.

He nodded and carried Katy back to the bedroom, where he eased her down into her crib and covered her. She sighed in her sleep and stuck her fist in her mouth, sucking on it. Jesse ran a hand over her soft curls before checking on Max and tiptoeing out of the room. Valentina took him by the hand and led him back to their room, where she shut the door and pounced on him.

"I believe you said you weren't done yet," she said as she nipped his lip.

Jesse grinned. "We've got all night."

"Then we should get started," she said as she kissed him long and deep.

His hands came around her waist, and he couldn't help but think his life was finally complete. The best thing that had ever happened to him was finding Valentina and the kids in his parking lot, and he was going to spend every day for the rest of his life making sure they were happy and loved, and never wanted to leave.

Epilogue

Six Months Later

"Valentina, we're going to be late," Jesse called from the front door.

"I'm coming," she yelled down the hall.

Mrs. Wilson patted his arm. "You don't worry about those precious babies. I know what I'm doing and I have your number in case of an emergency. The two of you have a nice time tonight."

"Thank you, Mrs. Wilson."

The librarian patted his arm once more before going down the hall toward the kids' room. Valentina rushed into the living room, one shoe on and one off, as she stuck a hoop in her ear. Her hair was flowing down her back and the little black dress she'd put on hugged her pregnant belly. Jesse couldn't remember ever seeing a more beautiful woman.

Valentina fastened her earring and slipped on her shoe before giving him a dazzling smile. "I'm ready if you are."

Jesse held out his hand and she rushed to his side. He led her down the stairs and helped her into the truck. They weren't going far, just the Italian place over on Main, but he'd booked a special reservation, asking for a private table in a cozy corner. Everything had to be perfect tonight.

His heart was racing as they entered the restaurant. The tabletops were covered in checkered cloths and candles flickered on them. The hostess seated them at a table in the front corner, the potted palms surrounding it giving it a hint of privacy. Valentina looked around in curiosity as she settled into her seat.

"Why do I feel like you're up to something?" she

asked.

"I just didn't want to share you tonight. You know every time we go out somewhere, people always come up and talk to us. I wanted you to myself for a little while."

"You're always so thoughtful and romantic," she said as she looked over her menu.

Jesse's palms were damp and he couldn't focus on the words in front of him. A server brought over some water and took their order.

"Can we have the dessert first?" Jesse asked.

"Dessert first?" Valentina asked.

"It's a special one," Jesse said, "so I want to make sure you have room for it."

She didn't look like she quite believed him but the server hurried off and returned a few minutes later with a slice of tiramisu. He set the dish down in front of Valentina and her eyes went wide when she looked down at it.

"Jesse…"

He came around the table and knelt at her feet, taking one of her hands in his. Jesse plucked the engagement ring from the dessert and held it up to her.

"Valentina, the last six months have been the happiest of my life. You and the kids mean the world to me, and I never want to go a day without you. Will you do me the honor of marrying me? Be mine, in all ways, now and forever?"

Her eyes misted with tears as she nodded her head. "Yes," she said in a near whisper. "I'll marry you."

Jesse slid the ring onto her finger and kissed her softly.

"I love you, Valentina. I think I have from the moment I found you in my parking lot."

"I love you too, and so do the kids. You're the best thing that ever happened to us."

They kissed again and Jesse reluctantly pulled away to reclaim his seat. Valentina held up her hand and admired her ring. It had taken him weeks to pick it out. He'd become well acquainted with the local jeweler before he'd finally found the right ring. He'd wanted tonight to be perfect, and now that she'd said yes, now that his family would be his permanently, he knew that every day would be better than the last.

"Thank you, Jesse," she said as she stared into his eyes.

"For what?"

"For proving that miracles really do happen. You're my miracle. I never thought I'd ever find a man who would love me, didn't think there were any good ones out there, but you proved me wrong. Every day with you has been a gift, and I will cherish every moment we spend together."

Jesse felt his eyes tear up, but he refused to cry. Men didn't cry, right?

He took her hand and held tight.

He didn't know what he'd ever done to deserve a woman as incredible as Valentina, or kids as awesome as theirs, but he would love and cherish them until he took his last breath.

Tessa's Hero (Blossom Creek 2)
Paige Warren

Tessa Milner never had much, but when she lost her mom, she lost everything. Her dad became a mean drunk and lost his job. What little the high school dropout makes bussing tables helps keep the lights on and food in the fridge, but she has little hope of ever escaping. When her dad takes things too far, and Tessa ends up in the hospital, she finds a hero in an unlikely place. A man she's had a crush on since she was a kid, someone she's always idolized. And now he's here, by her side, and doesn't seem ready to leave anytime soon.

Dr. Morgan Hilliard has felt drawn to Tessa ever since he first noticed the woman she was becoming, with curves that begged to be touched. He's wanted to ask her out more times than he can count, but because of their age difference, he's tried to keep his distance. The small town of Blossom Creek might be accepting of an interracial couple, but their nearly twenty year age gap is sure to set tongues wagging. Now things are different. Tessa needs him, whether she'll admit it or not, and Morgan will do anything to keep her safe -- even something as crazy as marrying her.

Chapter One

Tessa Milner slowly backed away from her dad as he swayed on his feet, a nearly empty bottle of whiskey clutched in his hand. Ben Milner was a mean ass drunk, and ever since Tessa's mom had died a few years ago, the drinking had gotten worse. He'd once been a handsome man, his red hair thick and curly, his eyes bright and kind. Now his hair looked like it hadn't been washed in weeks and his eyes were lifeless. When Nicole Milner died, her husband's heart had died too. Her mom had been beautiful. A mocha goddess who'd smiled and laughed all the time, bringing out the best in everyone. But when her mom died, so did the laughter in the house, and the love. Tessa didn't recognize the man in front of her anymore. The guy who'd carried her on his shoulders or played tag with her was long gone. A monster now resided in his body.

Her dad let the rusted screen door slam behind him as he staggered across the sagging front porch. His boots kicked up paint chips from the peeling boards under his feet. Peaches, their beagle, was resting on the top step. A twisted smile crossed her dad's face before he pulled back his booted foot and kicked Peaches off the top step, the dog yelping as she went airborne and tumbled to the ground below. Peaches whimpered and couldn't seem to get up.

Tessa's heart pounded as tears fell down her cheeks, and she wanted to rush to Peaches, but she knew better. Her dad nearly fell down the stairs as he came after her, and not for the first time, Tessa wished he'd fall and break his damn neck. Anything to end the torment. She couldn't run because that would only make it worse when he did catch her, and he always caught her. For an uncoordinated drunk, he could move damn fast, and he was downright vicious on the best of days.

"Pretty girl like you could get us out of this mess," her dad slurred.

She knew exactly what he was asking, and she wasn't about to do it. Tessa shook her head and took a step back.

"Stan would treat you right," her dad said.

Stan Trotter was nearly sixty, and he'd been eyeing Tessa since she'd turned fifteen. Sick perv. The man had always made her skin crawl, with his inappropriate touches and innuendo, and now her dad wanted to sell her to the man. They'd hatched some plan over drinks, twenty thousand dollars for Tessa to crawl into Trotter's bed and obey his every command, but Tessa refused to go along with it. She wasn't whoring herself out just so her dad could live a better life while she suffered at Stan's hands.

"No, Daddy," she said.

"You little bitch." Her dad lurched forward, his hand a blur as he lashed out toward her.

Pain exploded across her cheek, but she remained upright. Her dad came at her again and caught her on the side of the head with his closed fist and she saw stars. Tessa swayed, but refused to go down. If he got her on the ground, the real torment would begin. A few more blows to her face and ribs, and he seemed to lose interest in her, the fight draining out of him. He tipped up his nearly empty bottle, draining it dry, then tossed it into the yard, where it clinked against the other discarded bottles, before staggering back into the house, probably looking for another drink. With some luck, he'd pass out.

Tessa openly cried as she pulled Peaches into her arms, ignoring her own aches and pains. She loaded the beagle into her rusted car, snuck into the house to grab her purse, and drove to the vet clinic in town. Dr. Hilliard had treated Peaches before, and Tessa hoped he'd be able to help her now. She didn't know if she had enough money for the visit, but maybe he would work with her on payments. She couldn't let her dog suffer. Peaches had been her best friend for the last six years, and she deserved a better life than she had now. They both did.

Tears blurred her vision as she pulled to a stop in front of the clinic. It was nearing five, but the open sign was up. She pulled Peaches from the car and carried her into the clinic, ringing the bell on the front counter. She knew this late in the day, most of the staff would be gone, but she'd seen Dr. Hilliard leaving the clinic sometimes hours after closing time.

"Dr. Hilliard!" she called out.

A door opened and he stepped out of the back, his lab coat still on and his hair mussed, as if he'd been running his hands through it. The man was sexier than anyone had a right to be, with his dark hair and neatly trimmed beard, and when those hazel eyes looked at you, it almost felt like you were the most important person in the world. Or maybe it had something to do with the crush she'd had on him half her life.

"What's wrong with Peaches?" he asked, coming closer.

"Dad kicked her off the porch. She wouldn't get up and I'm worried something might be broken."

The doctor looked at the dog, stroking her head and ears, before really taking a look at Tessa. When he did, his eyes narrowed and some not so very nice words spilled out of his mouth.

"It seems the dog isn't the only one he abused today," the doctor said.

"I'm fine," Tessa assured him, having gone through far worse at her father's hands. "It's Peaches I'm worried about."

Dr. Hilliard took Peaches from her and carried the beagle into an exam room, with Tessa on his heels. He looked the dog over then took her down the hall for an x-ray. When he came back, he had a grim expression on his face.

"Peaches has a fractured rib, which is probably why she didn't want to stand up. It's going to be painful for her to move, and breathing might hurt her until it heals. I can give you some pills for the pain, but you should watch her closely. In the next few days, if you think she's getting worse, bring her back and I'll see if I missed something. There's quite a bit of swelling right now, so smaller fractures might be harder to discern."

"Thank you, Dr. Hilliard." She stroked her beloved pet's head.

"Tessa, how old are you now?" Dr. Hilliard asked. "Old enough to be on your own, aren't you?"

"I'm nineteen. I'll be twenty in a few months." She looked up at him. "You wonder why I stay, don't you?"

"It crossed my mind."

"I don't make very much. The only job I was able to find was bussing tables at the Golden Apple."

Something that looked like anger flared in his eyes. "You're working where?"

Her cheeks flushed. "The Golden Apple. I don't get on stage though, I just clean the tables."

Working in a strip club hadn't been her first choice, but the diner hadn't had any openings, and neither had any of the other restaurants around town. She'd missed too much school to graduate, and not many people were looking to hire a high school dropout. She wanted to get her G.E.D., but there hadn't been time.

"Does your father know where you're working?" he asked.

"Daddy doesn't care as long as I can pay for his alcohol. Or rather, as long as he can when he steals my money. I had a jar hidden in my room, trying to save up enough to get out of there, but he found it and spent every penny."

"Tessa, it's not safe for you to be there. You or Peaches."

He wasn't telling her anything she didn't already know, especially with her father pushing Stan Trotter on her. She'd started locking her door at night, after the time he'd invited the man over for drinks and Stan had wandered into her room while she was sleeping. She'd woken to his hand under her gown, stroking her where he had no right to touch. Tessa knew better than anyone how dangerous it was to live at home, but what other choice did she have? She didn't make enough to pay rent anywhere in town.

She stroked Peaches again, and worried about her dog. If her dad had kept drinking after she left, and he wasn't passed out on the couch, there was no telling what kind of mood he'd be in. If he kicked the dog again, could it kill her?

"Dr. Hilliard, I have no right to ask this, but would you take Peaches home with you? Just for a few days until she's doing a little better?"

"Tessa…"

"Please. I don't think I have enough money to cover the visit today and boarding her too, but it's not safe for her at home tonight."

"I'll take her home," he said softly. "She can stay

as long as you need her to."

"Thank you." Her eyes misted with tears as she kissed her beloved beagle. "You be a good girl for the doctor."

Peaches wagged her tail.

"Tessa, are you going to be okay?" Dr. Hilliard asked.

"I'll be fine."

"You know I have to report this visit to the sheriff. He'll have to cite your dad for animal cruelty."

Tessa blanched, knowing that was a really bad idea. He'd blame her for it, and probably take it out of her hide. But she wasn't going to ask the doctor to break the law, no matter the consequences for her. It wouldn't be the first time her dad came after her, and she doubted it would be the last. As long as Ben Milner continued to drink, she would suffer at his hands.

"Are you all right, Tessa?" Dr. Hilliard asked, concern shining in his eyes.

"F-fine. I'd better get home. I have a shift to work tonight and need to get ready."

The look on his face clearly said he didn't believe her, but he didn't stop her from walking away. Tessa got into her car and drove back to the house, hoping her dad was passed out, or gone for the night. Her stomach cramped as she thought about the sheriff visiting, but she'd deal with it when the time came. As late as it was, he probably wouldn't show up until morning. For now, she needed to get her head screwed on straight. Working at the Golden Apple was no joke. Yeah, she just bussed tables, but it didn't stop the clientele from copping a feel and trying to convince her to do more. Like take off her clothes or visit the back rooms with them.

She was still clinging to her virginity, and the

thought of those men -- any men except one -- touching her sickened her, but she needed the money. Her check was all that kept the lights on some months, or any food in the house. When her dad had been released from his job with a severance package, she'd convinced him to pay off what little remained on the house -- as crappy as the place was, it was better than living on the streets -- and then he'd blown the rest on alcohol.

She pulled down her bumpy driveway and breathed a sigh of relief when she didn't see her dad's car. Hurrying inside, she got ready for work and drove to the Golden Apple. It was chaos backstage as the girls got ready for their performances, among other things. Tessa quickly tied her apron around her waist and started wiping down the empty tables. She felt exposed in her work clothes, a barely there shirt and shorts that showed the curve of her ass, but the uniform was required of anyone working the floor. Unless they opted to wear less, like some of the topless servers.

Tessa might work in this place, but it didn't mean she was ready to rip her clothes off for money. She didn't think badly of the girls who did. She knew they made great money, and some really seemed to enjoy the attention. But the first man who saw her naked would be the man she gifted with her virginity, and she wanted the moment to be special. Maybe she was stupid to think that way.

"Tessa!" her boss yelled across the floor. "Table in the corner."

She hauled her ass across the floor to the darkened corner and began clearing the table. She'd just placed the last glass in her tub when a hand gripped her around the waist and hauled her back against a rounded stomach. Her skin crawled and she tried to pull away.

"You're going to be mine, little girl. Might as well stop fighting it now."

Her blood froze in her veins. "I am not now, nor will I ever be yours."

She turned to face Stan Trotter and fought not to throw up on his shoes when he leered at her. His gaze caressed every inch of her and he licked his fat lips as he focused on her barely contained breasts. Tessa backed up into the table behind her and Stan followed. He reached out to trail a hand down her arm and she shivered in revulsion.

"I'm going to be so good to you," he said. "I can't wait to have you under me."

Throwing up was sounding better and better. She pulled free of his grasp, grabbed her tub, and hurried away, her heart pounding in her chest. He seemed so certain that she'd be his, no matter how many times she told him no. It made her scared, wondering just how far he'd go to have her.

Tessa finished the rest of her shift and went home, keeping an eye on her rearview mirror the entire way. She wouldn't put it past the creep to follow her, but thankfully she was alone on the road. When she reached her house, her dad's car was back and all the lights were off. Creeping into the house, she tiptoed to her room, locked her door and stripped out of her clothes, then took a quick shower before falling into bed.

No matter how exhausted she was, sleep was a long time coming. Fear made her stomach clench and she knew that Dr. Hilliard had been right. She needed to get out before it was too late. If it wasn't already.

Chapter Two

Morgan Hilliard knew something was horribly wrong when he saw the sheriff's SUV, both deputies, and an ambulance go flying by his office. He watched them head down the street then turn left toward the poorer side of town. He didn't doubt that whatever call they were answering it was bad. He hoped whoever was sick or injured would make it.

Peaches, Tessa's beagle, sat at his feet waiting for him to open the office. She'd been a great dog all night, even though he could tell she missed Tessa. She gave a beagle yodel and he smiled, unlocking the door and ushering her inside. Morgan stepped through the door, flicking on the lights. Peaches followed him past reception and down the hall to his office. He kept a dog bed along the wall for patients who needed to be watched closely and Peaches made herself at home on it. Morgan pulled out a rawhide from the package he kept in his office and tossed it to Peaches.

He pulled up his schedule on his computer and sighed. It was going to be a long ass day. He didn't have any surgeries scheduled, but it was back-to-back appointments, which was a little odd for such a small town. He kept busy, making more than enough to cover the bills and pay his employees well, but it didn't escape his notice that the owners of almost every pet on the list were single females.

Word was out around town that he wasn't *just* a vet, but the grandson and heir of Patrick Hilliard, the owner of several sports teams and a multi-millionaire. Ever since the news had hit town, Morgan hadn't had any peace from the female population. He'd always done all right with the ladies, when he took time off from school and work to bother dating, but this was different. They didn't want him for him, they just wanted the money.

"Thanks a lot, Grandpa," he muttered.

Ever since his grandfather had had a heart attack at the office, he'd been putting things into place in case he kicked the bucket. One of those things was apparently publicly naming Morgan as his sole heir. The local paper had picked up the story and run it on the front page. Not that Morgan gave a shit about the money. Most people didn't know that he'd been given a trust on his eighteenth birthday that he'd used to fund his college and the start-up for his clinic, and still had money to spare. He'd rather have his grandfather around for another forty years, but the man was nearing seventy and his health wasn't what it used to be.

He glared at the computer screen, wishing he could just cancel all of his appointments for the day. He already knew what to expect. A lot of flirting and giggling, some light touches, and too many low-cut shirts. This wasn't the first day he'd been through this, and he doubted it would be the last. Honestly, he felt sorry for the pets who were being dragged in that were more than likely perfectly healthy and would be terrified of coming to the clinic. It was abuse in his opinion, and he couldn't stand it when people abused their animals.

He glanced at Peaches and wondered how Tessa was faring. He hadn't given her a bill last night, and he'd make sure reception didn't send one out. Poor girl had enough to deal with already. He was a little surprised some young guy hadn't snapped her up and whisked her away from the nightmare she was living in. Tessa was easily the most beautiful girl in town, with her light mocha skin and all those damn curls.

Her eyes were wide and expressive, and her smile could light up a room, the few times he'd actually seen her smile.

If he weren't nearly twenty years her senior, he'd have made a play for her. The way she handled Peaches and always put the dog before her own needs, told him everything he needed to know about her. Despite the hand life had dealt her, she was kind and thought of others first. At least, that's how she'd appeared the times she'd brought Peaches in or when he saw her around town. It wasn't uncommon for Tessa to help the elderly, or give a kind word to someone. He hadn't thought much of her in her younger years, except acknowledging she was a sweet girl. But the year she'd turned seventeen, everything had changed. She'd blossomed overnight, with curves in all the right places. He wasn't proud of himself for lusting after a young girl, but he was a man and he noticed things like an attractive woman.

Morgan got his day started, seeing patient after patient, and trying to politely brush off every advance thrown his way. Maybe he should just tell everyone he was gay, but then he'd probably just have the men in town hitting on him. The first few hours of the day passed quickly, and he crept into his office for a short break before the next round of patients arrived. With back-to-back appointments, a lunch break might not happen.

Jeanie, his nurse, came in with a stack of files. The next set of patients for the day. He suddenly felt exhausted and wanted to crawl back into bed and stay there for a few days. Hell, he couldn't even remember the last time his dick had gotten attention other than his hand, and now thanks to his grandpa, he couldn't risk it. Even Jeanie had started looking at him differently. She wasn't as blatant as some of the women around town, but there was something different about her smile and the calculating gleam in her eye, as if she couldn't wait to get her hooks into him.

"Is that Peaches?" she asked, nodding toward the beagle.

"Yeah, Tessa brought her in last night. Seems Mr. Milner kicked Peaches down the stairs. I reported it to the sheriff last night and he was going to give Ben a citation for animal cruelty."

She tsked. "It's such a pity what happened."

Morgan frowned. "Peaches will be fine. She just needs to rest."

"I don't mean Peaches. I was referring to Tessa."

Morgan froze in mid-reach for his coffee. "What about Tessa?"

Jeanie's eyes went wide. "You didn't hear? Poor thing was rushed to the hospital this morning. It seems her daddy really went to town on her today."

The ambulance this morning. It had been going to Tessa's house. His heart pounded in his chest and his hand shook as he took a sip of his coffee. Was he responsible? Had Ben retaliated over the citation and taken it out on Tessa? Jesus. He was such an asshole that he hadn't even thought of that. If she'd been hurt because of him, he'd never forgive himself. His stomach churned, and he tried to focus on what Jeanie was saying.

"They arrested Ben Milner for assault, and word is out that Stan Trotter is trying to get her released into his care." Jeanie snorted. "I can just imagine the sort of care he'd give her."

"What do you mean?"

"Oh, please. That old perv has been lusting after

her since she was a kid. Everyone in town knows that."

Not everyone. He hadn't known. If that was true, he couldn't let the man get his hands on Tessa while she was vulnerable. Morgan stood and pulled off his lab coat before snatching his keys out of his desk drawer.

"Watch Peaches for me and cancel my appointments this afternoon," he said.

"Where are you going?" Jeanie demanded, her hand on her hip.

"I'm going after Tessa," he said.

"Morgan, I'm sure the sheriff can handle the situation. I know you're watching her dog and you've always had a soft spot for the poor girl, but let the law handle it."

He couldn't. If he'd said something last night, done something differently, then maybe Tessa would be fine right now. If he'd pulled his head out of his ass the first time he'd realized she was a grown woman, then maybe none of this would have ever happened. Or if he, or anyone, had paid closer attention to what was going on in her home for who knows how long, if someone had stepped forward, they could have ended her suffering a long time ago. He could have saved Tessa and Peaches. Everyone thought he felt sorry for her? That he thought of her as a little child? Hell, he'd been fighting his reaction to Tessa for the last two years, telling himself he was perverted for getting hard whenever she was nearby. He was surprised no one had ever noticed the tent in his pants when he was around Tessa.

He didn't know what he'd say or do when he got to the hospital, but he'd do whatever was necessary to make sure Stan Trotter didn't get his hands on her. Morgan felt like such an idiot for leaving her defenseless, knowing she was in a bad situation. Hell, everyone around town knew her dad was a mean ass drunk, and yet no one had ever stepped in to stop the abuse. He was sickened by the fact he'd stood by and let it happen for so long.

At the hospital he rushed inside and went straight to the ER triage.

"I need to see Tessa Milner," he said.

When the nurse looked up, he nearly groaned. *Anyone but her.*

Sadie's eyes lit up and she smiled brightly. "Morgan! It's so good to see you. I've been hoping you'd stop by so we could talk about that second date."

There wasn't going to be a second date. There shouldn't have even been a first date. He'd tried to be kind about it, and then had just avoided her as much as possible, but the woman wasn't taking a hint.

"I'm here to see Tessa," he said again.

Her smile dimmed a little. "That poor girl. We had to move her to a more secure room once she came out of surgery. She's on the second floor in room 208, but I don't know that the sheriff will let you in there. I didn't realize you were such good friends with Tessa."

"Thanks for your help, Sadie."

Before she could question him further, he took off for the elevators. Tessa's room was easy to find with the sheriff, two deputies, and an irate Stan Trotter in the hall outside her door. Morgan clenched his hands into fists, wanting nothing more than to knock out the asshole who was trying to take advantage of Tessa. It might have been a while since he'd been in a fight, but he'd done plenty of boxing in high school and college, and he figured he could lay the man out.

The sheriff's eyebrows rose when he saw him.

"Dr. Hilliard, didn't realize you were coming by."

"I heard about Tessa."

Sadness clouded the sheriff's eyes. "She's not awake, but you can go in and see her."

"Why does he get to go in and I don't?" Trotter demanded. "She's mine! If you don't believe me, ask her father. We have an arrangement."

Morgan's stomach soured at the thought of just what type of arrangement those two might have come up with. Brushing past the sheriff, he entered the room and his heart nearly stopped. Machines beeped and wires were everywhere. Tears pricked his eyes as he saw the bruises and cuts on her beautiful face. Fingerprints marred the skin on her arms, and he wondered what other damage there was. Sadie had mentioned surgery.

Morgan stepped further into the room and settled on the chair next to her bed. Gently, he took her hand in his, mindful of her IV. Her fingers were cold and lifeless as he lifted them to his lips and softly kissed them. It was the closest he'd ever allowed himself to get, and now he was wishing he could change things. He should have gotten her out of that house, away from her dad. He should have been a man and taken care of the woman who affected him like no other, but he'd been scared, worried about what people would think. The color of her skin didn't matter, but she was nineteen and he was thirty-eight. It was bound to cause gossip. Even if he hadn't claimed her the way he wanted, he should have found a way to get her out of there.

"I'm so sorry, Tessa. I was such a coward, and it could have cost you your life. I need you to fight, to get better and open those beautiful brown eyes."

The sheriff stepped into the room. "Short of

throwing Trotter in jail for disturbing the peace with all his blustering, I don't know how to get rid of the man."

"I'll be happy to toss him out a window."

The sheriff chuckled. "Tempting. I never did like that asshole. He won't give me the details of the supposed arrangement he has with Tessa's dad, but I'm betting it's not good."

"She can't leave the hospital yet anyway, right?"

"The doctor said she'll be here about a week in recovery. There was some internal bleeding, she has a concussion, and quite a few stitches. You can't see it, but he sliced her ribs with a knife after beating the hell out of her."

"Is it because of me?" Morgan asked softly. "Because I reported him for animal cruelty?"

"You can't blame yourself, Morgan," the sheriff said. "And I honestly don't know what started it. Ben isn't talking, other than to repeatedly say she's a disobedient child who needs to be punished, and Tessa hasn't woken up yet."

A woman in a suit stepped into the room, a clipboard in her hand.

"Sheriff, do you know if Tessa has insurance? I need to get some information down to billing."

Morgan growled. "She's lying here unconscious and you're worried about getting paid? Get the hell out!"

The woman blanched, stammered an apology, and bolted out the door.

The sheriff chuckled. "That's one way to get rid of the leeches. But the hospital is going to want their money. Tessa's old enough she'll be held responsible for her bill, even if her old man put her in here."

"She said she didn't have enough money to pay for Peaches' vet visit last night and you think she has the cash to pay a hospital bill for a week-long stay plus whatever else they tack on there?"

The sheriff shrugged. "I'm sure they'll make payment arrangements or something."

"I'll take care of it," Morgan said softly, his gaze going back to Tessa.

"Not to pry or anything, doc, but shouldn't you be at work?" the sheriff asked.

"I cancelled my afternoon appointments."

The sheriff rocked back on his heels, a thoughtful look in his eyes. "Are you here because you feel guilty or for another reason?"

"Maybe a little of both."

"That girl could use a hero right about now. Think you're up for the task?" the sheriff asked.

"I'll be anything she needs me to be. If I hadn't kept my distance, maybe this wouldn't have happened. But I stupidly thought our age difference was too much to overcome. Why didn't anyone help her in all this time? Were we all blind to it, or just indifferent?"

The sheriff patted his shoulder. "You'll catch some grief from people, especially with you being the town's number one bachelor, but don't listen to them. You've got to follow your heart, doc. Life is too short to live with regrets."

He was starting to learn that the hard way. He just hoped that Tessa could forgive him. Whatever it took, he would protect her. He'd always felt like she was his, even though he'd tried to deny his feelings, but he wasn't running away anymore. From this moment on, he would be the man Tessa deserved, the kind of man who would fight for what he wanted. And he wanted Tessa.

Chapter Three

Tessa hated the hospital bed she'd been stuck in for over a week. The only bright spot was the frequent visits from Dr. Hilliard. The first time she'd opened her eyes, he'd been slumped over her bed, his head resting near her hip as he held her hand and slept. Emotion had welled inside of her and nearly choked her, and she'd been worried that she was hallucinating. A nurse had bustled into the room, happy to see her awake, and had informed her that the vet had been by her side every night and even stopped in during his lunch breaks.

Tessa couldn't understand why he'd been here so much, but she'd enjoyed his company. He'd held her hand a lot, and always asked if she needed anything. It was strange, having the man she'd fantasized about for so long suddenly paying attention to her. He'd always been kind when she'd taken Peaches to his clinic, but he'd always maintained a certain distance. She didn't understand what changed, or what it all meant.

She heard shouting in the hall near her room.

"That girl belongs to me!"

A shiver raked her spine as she recognized the voice of Stan Trotter.

"If *that girl*, as you call her, belongs to anyone, it's Dr. Hilliard."

Her cheeks warmed at the nurse's words. Did they really think she belonged to the handsome vet? She couldn't think of anything she'd love more, but what would a successful man like Morgan Hilliard want with her? She came from the poor side of town, had dropped out of high school, and was going nowhere fast in life. A man like him could have any woman he wanted, and she knew there were plenty around town trying to catch his eye. Sophisticated women with college educations, every hair in place and perfectly dressed. The kind of woman who would make him proud.

She heard more shouting in the hall and then footsteps running toward her room. Stan Trotter sounded furious and she clutched her covers tight, fearing he'd burst through her door at any moment. The hospital staff said she was being released tomorrow, and Tessa worried what would happen to her. She could live in her home while her dad rotted in jail, but she had a feeling a door lock wouldn't keep Trotter at bay much longer. He saw her as his property. There was more shouting and booted steps running toward her room, and then Trotter's voice faded.

A nurse popped into the room, a strained smile on her face. "Honey, the police asked us to keep Stan Trotter out of your room since he's been talking crazy about owning you, but I'm getting a little worried. Do you have anyone you can stay with when you're released tomorrow?"

"No. It's just me now that Dad's in jail."

The nurse didn't look comforted by Tessa's words. "It's almost dinner. I bet that handsome vet of yours will be by to visit."

Tessa flushed. "He's not mine."

"Oh, honey. Trust me, he's yours if you want him. The doctors had to practically throw him out just to get him to go to work while you were still unconscious."

"I'm sure I'll be fine," she said, even if she didn't believe the words. No, as long as Stan Trotter was around, she wouldn't be fine. Far from it. If what her dad said was true, he'd already accepted money for her.

The nurse patted her hand, but still looked worried. "You just buzz the nurse's station if you need anything. It's about time for that handsome vet of yours to stop by. Maybe you should talk to him about Mr. Trotter. I bet he could come up with a solution for you."

Maybe, but she hated to burden Dr. Hilliard. No, he'd told her to call him Morgan. He'd been so kind to her, so attentive. The last thing she wanted to do was take advantage of him. It was bad enough Peaches had stayed with him so long. Tessa was anxious to leave the hospital and get on with her life, as best she could. She didn't even know if she still had a job. The Golden Apple wasn't the type of place that would hold your spot even for a medical emergency. When she hadn't shown up, it was likely they'd hired someone else.

Her future was looking rather bleak at the moment. But no matter what, she wouldn't let it get her down. After everything she'd survived, she'd make it through this too. Somehow. She'd just have to work hard at finding another job. The utilities were paid through end of the month, and she always kept Ramen stocked for the weeks there wasn't enough grocery money. It wouldn't be a fun few weeks, but she could do it.

At least she wouldn't have to avoid her father's fists. Though there was Stan Trotter to deal with. She knew he'd do anything he could in order to drag her off. He wanted her, had always wanted her, and now that he'd paid her father he thought he had a right to her. If she told the sheriff, maybe he could stop Trotter from taking her.

She'd kept silent so far, too scared to speak out. And maybe a little embarrassed that her father thought so little of her.

The door to her room opened and Morgan stepped inside, a smile on his handsome face. He was dressed in scrubs, which meant he'd come straight from the clinic. "I hear you get to go home tomorrow," he said as he eased into the chair next to her bed.

"That's what they tell me."

"Do you need a ride home from the hospital?" he asked. "I could take off and come pick you up."

"That's really sweet of you, Morgan, but I've already taken up so much of your time. Your patients must hate me with all the work you've missed."

He took her hand. "You let me worry about that."

"Morgan, why are you here? I know my dog is one of your patients, but do you visit all the owners in the hospital?"

He smiled a little. "No, I don't. Only the special ones."

Her insides warmed at his words, but she tried not to read too much into it. Should she confide in him about Stan Trotter? Maybe get his opinion on how to handle the situation? Morgan was a very intelligent man, probably far smarter than her. He was older and had seen more of the world. Tessa had lived her entire life in Blossom Creek, on the poor side of town.

"Morgan, can I ask you something?" she asked.

"Of course."

"It *is* illegal to buy someone, right?"

His gaze sharpened and his hand tightened on hers. "*Buy* someone?"

"You know, like if a man wanted a woman in his bed, but she'd refused, he couldn't give her father money for her, could he?"

"Your father *sold* you to Stan Trotter? Is that what you're telling me?" he demanded, his voice harsh.

Tessa swallowed hard and nodded hesitantly. "It's why he beat the hell out of me. He informed me that morning that it was a done deal and Stan would be coming to pick me up. He said I was supposed to do whatever Stan wanted. I refused."

"Jesus, Tessa. Why didn't you say something to the sheriff? I know he asked what happened that morning."

"I was scared," she said softly. "Any time I've tried to stand up for myself or protect myself in any way, it's always backfired. What if the sheriff didn't do anything and Stan Trotter got angry with me? If he forced me to go with him, I'd be at his mercy."

Morgan blew out a breath and focused on her again. "Sweetheart, that man is not now, nor is he ever, getting his hands on you. I'm calling the sheriff and you're going to tell him exactly what you told me. Yes, it is completely illegal for your father to sell you or for Trotter to purchase you. They should both get jail time for it."

Tessa nodded and Morgan pulled out his cell phone. The conversation didn't last long and it only took the sheriff fifteen minutes to show up in her room. His expression was troubled.

"Tessa, why didn't you tell me about this before?" the sheriff asked after she'd explained everything to him.

"She was frightened," Morgan said. "You can get more charges added to her father and arrest Trotter, right?"

"All I have is Tessa's word based off something her father told her. And Stan Trotter claiming to have some arrangement with the man, but he won't say what. He never mentioned money. I'll have to investigate before we can file charges, unless her dad will confess to the crime."

"She's being released tomorrow," Morgan said.

"Remember that talk we had?" the sheriff asked Morgan. "Now's the time."

Morgan nodded and waited a moment for the sheriff to leave before he focused on Tessa again. She didn't have any idea what conversation they'd had, but it had obviously been about her. Morgan caressed her hand and seemed to be thinking awfully hard. She hoped whatever he had to say that it wasn't bad news. She didn't think she could handle much else right now.

"Tessa, it's not safe for you to go home tomorrow," Morgan said. "I know you're independent and probably want to take care of yourself, but you need help right now."

"My dad is all I have and he's in jail."

"No, sweetheart. Your dad isn't all you have. You have me. When I pick you up tomorrow, we're going to your house so you can get a few things, and then I'm taking you to my place."

"Your place?" she asked, dumbfounded. Why was he taking her home with him? And why did he call her sweetheart? Tessa's head was spinning, and nothing made sense.

"I'm not explaining this very well, am I?" he asked.

Tessa shook her head. "I don't understand why you care what happens to me. We've barely spoken except when Peaches has had an appointment, and even then you're always distant but polite. I'm no one to you, and yet you've been here every day. What's going on, Morgan? I thought it was odd enough you didn't want me to call you Dr. Hilliard, but…"

"Tessa, I want to take care of you. I want you

under my roof where I can watch over you and keep you safe."

Her cheeks warmed. "And is that all you want?"

He smiled a little. "I won't lie. I'm attracted to you, have been for a while, even when I told myself that was all kinds of fucked up. But I'm not asking you to share my bed. You can have your own room and bathroom. I just need to know that you're safe and taken care of. It's important to me."

He might not be asking her to share his bed, but she'd gladly to do it. The only reason she'd held onto her virginity so long was because no one ever compared to him, not in her eyes. Despite her aches and pains, the thought of Morgan Hilliard's hands on her was enough to heat her from the inside out. The fact he wasn't trying to take advantage of her nearly brought tears to her eyes. No one had ever been so sweet to her before, or cared what happened to her. "I'll stay with you," she said softly.

He kissed the back of her hand. "I'd better run to the store and make sure I have everything you need. I'll be back in the morning to see if they've released you yet."

"Would you… would you go to my house and pack my things? I don't think I can enter that house right now. Trotter might be watching the place."

Morgan nodded.

"I don't know if the door is locked or not. I don't have my purse or anything. It's all in my room," she said.

"I'll take care of everything, Tessa. You just focus on getting better."

"Thank you, Morgan. It really means a lot to me. More than you could ever know."

He stood and brushed a kiss against her

forehead. "You rest. Have the nurses call me if you need anything."

She watched him walk away and felt a little like Alice falling down the rabbit hole. Successful, gorgeous, kind Dr. Hilliard actually found her attractive? And she would get to live with him, at least for a little while? She pinched her arm to see if she was dreaming. "Tessa, whatever you do don't screw this up," she muttered to herself. "That is one fine man and you get to play house with him."

Chapter Four

The sheriff met Morgan at Tessa's house. On the off chance the place was locked, he didn't want someone to report him breaking and entering. He looked at the overgrown yard littered with empty bottles of alcohol, the rusted screen door, and paint that seemed to come off the house in chunks. The porch sagged and there were shingles missing on the roof. He'd known that Tessa lived in this part of town, but he had never dreamed her home was like this.

The sheriff tried the knob and it easily turned in his hand, the door creaking as it opened. They entered the house and the stench nearly knocked Morgan off his feet. The carpet squished under their feet and the scent of urine filled the air.

"Do you think a wild animal got in?" Morgan asked.

"Maybe," the sheriff said, "but be prepared for anything."

"Any luck on locating the money Trotter supposedly paid to Tessa's dad?" Morgan asked.

"Not yet. I pulled his bank records and there wasn't anything out of the ordinary. Just his government assistance checks going in. I petitioned the courts to get a copy of Trotter's financials, but I don't have them yet. If he accessed a large sum of money recently, it's possible he paid Ben Milner in cash. Which means all we have is Tessa's word of something she was told and not something she witnessed firsthand. And even if Trotter is claiming some sort of deal with Mr. Milner, we can't say for certain it's illegal. Not with what little Trotter has said."

"Fuck. I don't like the sound of that."

They located Tessa's room easily enough and

froze in the doorway. Her mattress had been sliced to ribbons and her clothes littered the floor, ripped to shreds. There was piss all over the walls and furniture, almost as if someone had been marking their territory. Morgan didn't understand how any one human or animal could have urinated so much.

"Just how far are you willing to go to protect that girl?" the sheriff asked.

"I'd take a bullet for her."

"Still have that state of the art security system in your home?"

"Yeah."

"Good. Make sure it's on all the damn time. You should notify your alarm company of the situation as well. We're obviously dealing with a very disturbed individual. Stan Trotter must want Tessa pretty damn bad."

"You think he did this?" Morgan asked.

"If he didn't, then I'm sure he paid someone to do it. He wanted her vulnerable and afraid. I have no doubt he planned to be here when she got home from the hospital, and he probably would have taken her whether she was willing or not."

"Is there nothing you can do?" Morgan asked.

"I have to follow the law and the procedures in place. I can't arrest someone just because my gut tells me they did it. I have to have evidence. There's enough piss in this place I might be able to get a court order to compare it to Trotter's DNA, but that would still only slap him with a vandalism charge."

Morgan picked up some of Tessa's clothes and shoes, checking the sizes. He made a mental note of them and slowly made his way back through the house. The sheriff used his phone to take pictures of everything, even going through Ben's room, and promised to write up a report before he left the office for the night. Samples would need to be taken and tested, but the sheriff would have to call someone in for that. Morgan hated that Trotter could possibly get away with everything. They needed to find that damn money. The fact it wasn't in the bank and wasn't in the house didn't bode well. Like the sheriff said, without evidence there wasn't a crime.

Morgan's stomach churned as he drove away from Tessa's house, vowing he would do everything in his power to make sure she never returned to that place. She deserved so much better. He went to one of those twenty-four hour stores that would have a little bit of everything and he selected some new clothes and shoes for Tessa, purchased any toiletries she might need, then made sure there would be enough food in the house. After he got home and put everything away, tucking Tessa's new things into the spare room closest to his bedroom, and the bathroom across the hall, he forced himself to eat dinner and relax for the rest of the night, but Tessa was never far from his thoughts.

He'd have her under his roof, just one room away. He wondered how long it would take for the rumor mill to get started. Would anyone believe they weren't sleeping together? It didn't bother him, but it wasn't fair to Tessa. She'd already been through enough without having to deal with nasty gossip, and if the treasure-hunting females in town thought she'd snatched their prize away, they'd make her life hell. Morgan didn't know what else to do though. He had to protect her from Trotter, at any cost.

Morgan stripped out of his clothes and stretched out on the bed. Tomorrow was going to be a busy day and he needed some rest. He hadn't slept much since he'd found out Tessa was in the hospital. Hell, until

Trotter was locked up, he'd probably sleep with one eye open.

His phone rang and Morgan picked it up on the second ring.

"Hello."

"It's the sheriff. I called the judge and he denied my request for a sample from Trotter to match to the urine at Tessa's house. He said just because the man was trying to take care of her didn't mean he was crazy."

Morgan cursed.

"Yeah, my thought is that Trotter has some connection with the judge, which doesn't bode well for us. If the courts aren't on our side, there's not a hell of a lot we can do to protect that girl. Not unless he slips up or her dad admits he sold her."

"She can stay here as long as she wants," Morgan said.

"Doc, the only way Trotter won't be waiting for her is if she stays there forever, so unless you have some plan I don't know about, I think we're screwed."

He could send her somewhere, but then she'd be on her own. And Morgan didn't like the thought of her out there somewhere by herself. Surprisingly, the idea of Tessa being in his home forever didn't freak him out like it should have. Just the thought of her in his bed every night was enough to make him hard. He silently cursed as he looked down at his dick, which was now standing at attention.

"I'll do whatever it takes to keep her safe," Morgan said.

"I figured you'd say that," the sheriff said. "I'll keep you posted, Morgan, and keep your eyes open. I don't trust Trotter for a second."

Morgan hung up and stared at the ceiling. He

didn't trust Trotter either. He didn't like the thought of the other man's hands on Tessa. Hell, he didn't like the thought of anyone's hands on Tessa. Well, except his. He would give anything to trace her curves and make her scream his name. Morgan had spent more time than he should have wondering how she'd taste. He'd love nothing more than to spread her legs and feast on her for hours, until she came so many times she was begging him to stop.

He groaned as his cock jerked in response to his wayward thoughts. Oh yeah, he'd love to taste the sweetness between her thighs, lap up all that cream, and then fill her with his cock. He'd pound into that tight pussy, owning every inch of her, as she begged him for more. He'd pump hard and deep, and not stop until he erupted inside of her, pouring every ounce of cum into her slick channel. Then he'd pull out and watch as their mingled release slipped out of that gorgeous pussy. He wanted to mark her as his, fill her so full of his cum she didn't doubt for a minute that she belonged to Morgan.

He damn near came just thinking about it. Pulling open the bedside table drawer, he grabbed the lube and slicked his palm before taking his shaft in hand. His callused hand was no substitute for Tessa's tight little body, but if he closed his eyes, he could almost picture her riding him, her tits bouncing as those dark eyes stared down at him, so full of passion. Her little pussy would be hot and wet, sucking him in deeper and deeper.

Morgan stroked faster as he imagined her nails scoring his chest. He didn't want to just mark her as his, he wanted her to mark him as hers. He wanted those claw marks. Hell, he wanted bite marks and anything else she wanted to do to him. As he thought about her pussy taking him deep, he groaned and shot his load all over his chest and abdomen. He laid there, a mess covering him. It was crazy to even think Tessa would crawl into his bed, but he wanted her there. More than he'd ever wanted anything.

It figured the one woman he wanted in this damn town was the one who didn't seem interested.

Rolling out of bed, he went and started the shower. He'd cleaned up his mess so many times after thinking about Tessa that he'd showered more in the last two years than he had in his entire life. The last thing that poor girl needed was him lusting after her. She had enough to deal with already and didn't need a horny vet added to the mix. But damn if it wasn't hard to look at her and not wonder just how good her lips would look wrapped around his cock.

The first time he'd noticed the changes in her, he'd gone on a date with the first woman who asked and tried to exorcise the demons. But it hadn't worked. Oh, he'd gotten off, but it hadn't taken his thoughts away from Tessa. Nothing ever seemed to manage that feat. He'd had a series of one-night stands, but they'd tapered off even before his grandfather's announcement. They left him empty and aching for what he truly wanted and would probably never have. Even though she'd been seventeen at the time, it would have been perfectly legal for them to be together. The age of consent in Texas was seventeen, but being so much older than her, he'd still felt like a dirty old man.

Now he wished he'd just said to hell with everyone and gone after what he wanted. If Tessa had been in his life the last two years, he could have protected her. Moving her into his house felt right, even if she was staying in a guest room. She belonged here, with him. He hoped she'd come to the same conclusion and decide to stay, but if she ever wanted to leave, he wouldn't stop her. No matter how much it fucking hurt to watch her walk out the door.

He could be domineering in the bedroom, but he tried to never be an asshole. He'd never keep Tessa against her will, but he'd do anything in his power to convince her to stay. And if it meant giving her multiple orgasms every day? Well, he certainly wouldn't complain.

Morgan rested his head against the shower tiles as his dick hardened again. *Fuck*! He needed to stop thinking about Tessa. Or more specifically, he needed to stop thinking about Tessa in his bed, or his head between her thighs, or his dick in her mouth. The woman was too damn tempting, and now she was going to be under his roof. Maybe he should restock the lube. He had a feeling it was going to be a rough time, with her so close and yet so far away.

Damn but that woman turned him inside out.

* * *

Tessa couldn't help but feel a flutter of excitement as Morgan ushered her into his house. Peaches greeted them at the door, her beagle anxious to see her. Tessa knelt and scratched the dog behind the ears while Morgan locked the door and set the alarm. Despite the fact she had a big, strong man in the house, and apparently a state of the art alarm system, Tessa wasn't convinced that either of those things would keep Trotter at bay.

Morgan's hand came to rest at her lower back and a shiver raked her spine at the contact. Being alone in the house with him, especially at night, was going to be difficult. She'd wanted him for as long as she could remember, probably since she'd turned thirteen and decided boys weren't quite so yucky after all. And now she was here, in his home. Just the two of them. If he gave her even the slightest indication he'd be open to sharing his bedroom with her, she'd be all over him. But he'd treated her kindly, courteously, and while he did always seem to be touching her, it was never anywhere inappropriate.

She was so damn confused. At the hospital, the way the nurses spoke, she'd thought maybe there was something between them. But he'd never once tried to kiss her anywhere other than her forehead, cheek, or hand. Was he the type of man who wanted the woman to make the first move? Or were they wrong and he really wasn't interested in her like that? Maybe he was just trying to do a good deed.

"Your room is this way," he said, taking her by the hand and leading her upstairs.

Tingles shot up her arm from the contact. She couldn't help the smile that crossed her lips at being so close to the sexy vet, and the knowledge that she'd be sleeping just down the hall from him. If ever he was going to see her as a woman, it was going to be now. Tessa would give anything for a night in his arms. She wanted him to show her what she'd been missing all her life, to make her body his in every way possible. She just didn't know how to ask for it. Or if she should. What if she scared him away?

He pushed open a door near the end of the hall and her breath caught in her throat. The furniture was oak and shone like honey in the dappled sunlight that filtered through the white curtains. A pastel patchwork quilt covered the bed, and a rose-colored rug covered the wood floor beside it. It was far more spacious than her room at home, and had a simple elegance to it. She was going to feel like a princess sleeping in a place like this.

"I put some clothes in the dresser and closet for you. There are some shoes in there too."

"You got my things?" she asked.

"Um, no. Everything is new."

She turned to him, puzzled. "You couldn't get into the house?"

"Tessa, maybe we should talk about it later? You've just gotten home from the hospital and I'm sure you'd like to rest."

"Morgan, I've been stuck in a bed for over a week. The last thing I want to do is rest. What aren't you telling me?"

He sighed and ran a hand through his hair. "Someone broke into your home and trashed the place. Your bedroom was destroyed. I couldn't bring your things here because they'd been torn apart and…"

"And?"

"Someone urinated all over your house and room, Tessa. If you ever move back there, you'll have to strip out the carpets and repaint the walls, and you're going to need new furniture."

She sank onto the edge of the bed. There was only one person she knew who would react that violently toward her, other than her father, who was rotting in a cell. Had Trotter hoped to scare her into going to him? She didn't doubt for one minute he was the one behind it. Maybe he'd thought by destroying everything she owned, she'd have no choice but to turn to him.

"I'll pay you back," she said softly.

"No, Tessa. I don't want you to worry about the money, okay? Just focus on healing and staying safe. I don't want you to feel like a prisoner here, but it would probably be best if you didn't leave the house on your own. The sheriff thinks Stan Trotter was behind it, but the judge wouldn't grant him a court order for a DNA sample."

"So, once again, he gets away with something because there's no proof," she said.

"Pretty much. Look, I know it sucks, but I'm going to do everything I can to keep you safe. If you want out of the house, you can go with me to the clinic. Or on my days off, we can go somewhere."

"I didn't realize when I agreed to come home with you that I would disrupt your life. As long as I'm here, you're stuck having an unwanted guest, and you're nice enough to feel obligated to entertain me. You've been so sweet to me, and I can't tell you how much I appreciate it, but it's not fair for you to put your life on hold. How are you going to go on dates while I'm here?"

Morgan came closer, stopping in front of her. He reached down and took her hands, gently lifting her to her feet. Tessa looked up at him, worried what she would find in his eyes. She'd expected resignation, not… there was a warmth there, something she'd never seen with anyone else before. His gaze caressed her face as his hand slid around her back, pulling her closer.

"I'm not putting my life on hold," he said, his tone brooking no argument.

Her heart thumped in her chest as her soft curves were pressed against his hard body. Tessa's hands slid up his arms, resting on his biceps. She felt the muscles flex under her fingertips, and she'd never been more tempted to remove the man's shirt. She'd be willing to bet his body was hard and sculpted. Morgan slowly lowered his head, giving her plenty of time to pull away, but Tessa wanted his kiss. She'd dreamed of that and so much more. The nights she'd lain awake, her body aching, it had been Morgan she'd wanted to feel inside of her.

His lips brushed against hers, softly at first, then more demanding. Tessa surrendered to him, lost to his taste, the feel of his arms around her, the scent of his musky cologne. Everything about Morgan drew her in and made her want more. He pulled her tighter against him and she felt the ridge of his cock press against her belly. Tessa trembled in his arms, her panties growing damp. An ache built inside of her, one that she knew only Morgan could satisfy.

He groaned as he rubbed against her, his tongue flicking against hers. To know that he wanted her the way she wanted him made everything feel perfect in her world, at least for the moment. Tessa knew she would give him whatever he wanted, because what she wanted most was him. She didn't care if it was only the one time. She needed him more than her next breath.

Tessa reached between their bodies and pressed her hand against his cock, sliding her palm up and down the ridge. Morgan growled into her mouth and backed her against the bed. His hand slid over the curve of her ass, his fingers stroking between her legs. Tessa gasped and her knees went weak.

Morgan pulled away, his chest heaving, his eyes dark with passion.

"I'm sorry, Tessa, I shouldn't have done that."

He was taking it back? The best kiss of her life?

"I'm not sorry," she said. "I didn't want you to stop."

Morgan groaned and closed his eyes, a pained expression crossing his face. Tessa boldly reached for him again, her hand palming him through the denim of his jeans. His eyes flashed open and the heat in their depths nearly scorched her.

He pulled her closer again, his hand delving between her legs, stroking her through her pants. "Are you wet for me, baby?"

"Yes," she said breathlessly.

"Do you want me to make you feel good?"

Tessa nodded, not trusting her voice.

Morgan popped open the button on her pants and slid down the zipper. His fingers grazed her belly as his hand slipped under the waistband of her panties. She felt her breath coming out in short pants as he stroked the wet lips of her pussy.

"Christ, Tessa! So smooth and wet."

A finger dipped inside of her, making her cry out. While he stroked in and out of her, his thumb teased her swollen clit. Tessa thought she might combust as heat coursed through her like molten lava. Morgan's other hand grabbed her ass, holding her still as he fucked her with his fingers. A kaleidoscope of colors burst across her vision as she came with a keening cry. Her thighs trembled as he stroked and rubbed until the last wave of pleasure had rolled through her.

"You're so damn beautiful," he said.

"More," she begged.

He gave a humorless laugh as his hand slipped free of her pants, her cream coating his fingers. He sucked them clean, his heated gaze fastened on her. "I shouldn't have even done this much. I brought you here to protect you and you aren't under my roof fifteen minutes before I'm unfastening your pants."

"You didn't do anything I didn't want you to do."

"Tessa, you can't say things like that to me. You have no idea how hard it is for me to walk away right now."

"Then don't. I'm not asking you to."

His forehead pressed to hers. "Baby, I want you, more than I've ever wanted a woman before. But you need to heal. The last thing you need right now is me pounding this sweet pussy until neither of us can walk."

His words made her whimper with need. She wanted that, so much.

"I'm walking out of here, Tessa, and I don't want you to follow me. I want to take more from you, more than I should. Hearing you beg me for it just makes it even worse."

She nodded. She didn't like it, but she did understand. But if he was already kissing her, if he'd already made her come, that meant that he did want her. And if he wanted her, she knew he'd come back for more. Maybe not right now, but it would happen. And that would have to be enough to sustain her for now.

He kissed her again, hard and swift, before bolting out of the bedroom. She heard the door to the room next to hers slam shut. At least she now knew where he slept. Tessa took a shuddering breath. Leaving her pants unfastened, she gathered some of her new clothes, like the cute outfit he'd brought to the hospital for her, and stepped across the hall to shower. She could smell her arousal and if anything, it turned her on more.

Tessa soaped her body, moaning as her fingers slid across her sensitive pussy. No one had ever made her come before, except her own hand. She could still feel his fingers inside of her, still taste him on her tongue. He'd made her come, but she still felt unsatisfied. She wanted his hard cock sliding inside of her. He'd said he wanted to pound her pussy, and she wanted that, so damn much. The way he'd touched her, the way he'd kissed her, had her feeling more like a woman than she'd ever felt before.

"I'm not giving up on you, Morgan," she said softly. "I want you, and I will damn well have you."

Tessa played with herself until she came again, but still she ached and throbbed, needing something only Morgan could give her. She only hoped he didn't make her wait forever. It had been two years since she'd been old enough to date the handsome vet, almost three years, and she was done waiting. Now that she knew he desired her, nothing was going to hold her back.

Chapter Five

Morgan groaned and banged his head on the wall. What the fuck had he been thinking? Oh, right. He hadn't been. He'd let his dick take over the second she was under his roof. *Way to go, asshole*. Now she was going to think he was like every other fucker out there, just after a quick screw. He could have that any time he wanted, if he dared be brave enough. He wouldn't put it past some of the women in town to either fake a pregnancy or get pregnant for real just to trap him into marriage. Well, to hell with that. He'd been quite content just using his hand. It had just been him and his palm for so long, he was surprised he could even remember what it felt like to be inside of a woman.

Until Tessa.

Her lips had tasted so sweet. Her pussy had been smooth as silk and so damn wet. She'd drenched his fingers before she even came, and he'd wanted like hell to strip her bare and feast on those succulent lips. He wanted her cream on his tongue as she came, screaming his name and writhing under him, begging for more. And he'd damn near taken what he wanted. The tang of her arousal had filled the air around them and it had nearly brought him to his knees.

He glared at his cock, still pressing against his pants, wanting to be set free. No, it didn't just want freedom, it wanted Tessa. His dick wanted to feel those slick walls clenching him tight as he drove into her, the force of every thrust sending her up on her toes as he got as deep as her body would allow. *Fuck*!

There was no way the monster in his pants was going to calm down if he didn't slow his thoughts. Morgan took deep breaths and tried to think of anything but Tessa. He mentally recited the periodic table, in order, then went through the steps of how to diagnose and treat parvo. By the time he'd thought of rectal exams and spaying cats, his cock had deflated enough that he felt safe leaving his bedroom.

The hall bathroom door was shut, and he could hear the shower running. As he went to pass by, he heard a moan that froze him in his tracks. His heart hammered in his chest as Tessa called out his name, obviously pleasuring herself under the hot spray.

"Jesus. I'm so fucked," he muttered, and nearly raced down the hall and down the stairs.

He'd known she'd be a temptation when he brought her here, but he'd never expected her to want him as badly as he wanted her. It had never crossed his mind that she thought of him as anything other than her vet, or maybe just an older man who was nice to her. He'd thought that if anything happened between them, he'd have to work for it. Now he had to wonder just how long Tessa had wanted him. When she teased that pussy at home, was it always his name she called out? Or had it only been today because of what happened between them?

The grandfather clock in the entryway chimed eleven o'clock. He tried to gather his scattered thoughts long enough to make lunch. Tessa would need good food to help her heal. Vegetables and good protein. His dick started to harden again. *Not that kind of protein, asshole.*

He grabbed some yellow and red bell peppers, slicing them. Morgan pulled out his favorite skillet and added some canola oil, turning on the burner. When the oil had warmed, he tossed in the peppers and some seasoning. He took an onion and garlic clove out of the pantry. He diced a fourth of the onion and all of the clove, then tossed the chunks in with the peppers.

While they sautéed, he started the water for some minute rice and took some chicken breasts out of the fridge. Slicing them thinly, he added them to the skillet.

By the time everything was finished and he was plating their food, Tessa made an appearance. Her corkscrew curls bounced with every step and he couldn't help but think she looked damn good in the sundress he'd picked out for her. Her feet were bare and he saw her toes were tipped with pink polish. Morgan stared, his pants growing tight again. *What the fuck*? Since when did a woman's feet turn him on?

Maybe he'd gone without sex for too damn long.

"I thought you might be hungry," he said. "It's not much. Just a little stir fry with some rice."

"It smells great," she said, smiling with a gleam in her eye that spoke of trouble.

Something told Morgan he was going to have to keep an eye on her for reasons other than her health, or Trotter. Morgan set their plates on the table and got two bottles of water from the fridge. He handed her a fork and napkin, then settled in the chair next to her.

Tessa took a bite and her eyes went wide. "This is really good."

He smiled. "I'm glad you like it. I wasn't sure what types of things you liked to eat."

Tessa shrugged. "Anything is fine. Since Mom died, it's mostly been Ramen noodles and boxed dinners. Couldn't really afford anything else with Dad's drinking habit. But at least there was food on the table. Most of the time."

"Damn, Tessa. Why didn't you ever ask for help?"

"Who was I supposed to ask? Besides, I don't need charity."

"Letting people help you isn't accepting charity. It's what friends and neighbors do for one another."

She bit her lip and didn't say anything. He didn't want to push her, but he hated that she'd had to live like that. It made his stomach sour, thinking he could have done something about her situation and hadn't. He'd been so caught up in his own issues, and running from their age difference, that he hadn't been a man and done the right thing. Everyone in town knew her dad was a mean drunk, and he'd seen bruises on Tessa more than once.

"I'm sorry," he said softly. "So damn sorry, Tessa."

She glanced at him, curiosity in her pretty brown eyes. "What for?"

"I should have done something. When I…"

"When you what?"

"The first time I noticed you the way a man notices a woman, you'd turned seventeen. You were old enough, according to the law, but I worried what people would think because of our age difference. If I hadn't been such a damn coward, if I'd gone after you, or at least called someone the first time I saw the bruises, then maybe you wouldn't be in this position right now."

Her gaze softened and she reached for his hand. "I don't blame you, Morgan. What happened to me is no one's fault but my dad's and Trotter's. Mostly my dad's fault. Before he turned to alcohol to numb the pain of losing Mom, he never would have done something like this. He never so much as raised his voice to me when I was little. It was only after Mom died that things changed. I think part of him died with her."

"I want to help you, Tessa. I truly did bring you

here only for that reason. What happened upstairs…" He shook his head. "I didn't mean for that to happen. You're dealing with enough already without me sticking my hand down your pants."

"And to think I put on a dress to make things easier for you," she said.

Morgan choked on his water. "What?"

"I like you, Morgan. I've always liked you. I've had a crush on you since I was thirteen. You don't have to keep apologizing for what happened. If I hadn't wanted you to touch me, I'd have told you."

Her gaze was earnest and he believed her, even if he did still feel bad about practically fucking her within minutes of her entering his house. He should have known that having her here would be too much temptation. He'd wanted her for so damn long, had jerked off to her countless times. And now she was here. And apparently willing to let him touch her whenever he wanted. Morgan wasn't sure if he should rejoice or be afraid.

They finished their lunch and Morgan cleared the table, loading the dirty dishes into the dishwasher. Tessa made herself comfortable in the living room and Morgan flicked on the TV. He handed her the remote, not having a clue what she liked to watch. It was amazing that he'd known her for so long, and yet there was little he really knew about her. He knew she was kind and always had a smile for everyone, that she was good to her dog, that she kissed like an angel and came apart in his arms so sweetly.

"What do you want for your future, Tessa?" he asked.

"My future?"

"Well, you can't want to work at the Golden Apple forever."

She snorted. "I'm pretty sure I don't have that job anymore. I need to call and make arrangements to get my last check."

"So what do you want to do?"

"You mean in a perfect world?" she asked. "I guess get my G.E.D. and either get an office job around town or maybe take some classes at the community college. I've never really had any options so I haven't thought about it much. I've mostly focused on getting by day to day."

"You didn't finish high school?" he asked.

"I had to drop out. With Dad drinking so much, he lost his job. I needed to work for us to survive. And even if I could have managed classes and working, I doubt the school would have turned the other way for very long, not when I showed up every day with bruises. The last thing I wanted was to end up in foster care. I've heard the horror stories of what happens. My dad might be a horrible drunk, but at least he didn't molest me."

"You have time to figure things out."

"Do I?" she asked. "I can't stay here hiding from Trotter forever, Morgan. If he doesn't give up, and I doubt that he will, he will eventually own me."

Morgan gripped her chin and forced her to look at him. "Do not *ever* say that again. Trotter will never get his hands on you. I won't let him."

"You can't stop him, Morgan. I don't think anyone can. He's well connected, not only in town but in the county. Hell, he probably has friends at the state level. No one is going to arrest him for anything, as much as I wish they would. No evidence, no crime, right? And you're never going to find that money. I'm sure he went to the house and took it. The way you found the place, that had to be his doing."

"We'll find a way, Tessa. I'm going to keep you safe."

"You want to know the worst part?" she asked softly.

"What's that, sweetheart?"

Her gaze met his, tears pooling in her eyes. "I saved myself all these years because no one ever measured up to you. If Trotter gets his hands on me, he won't just own me. He'll take my virginity too. It was supposed to be special, a gift for the right man."

The world tilted for a moment as Morgan processed her words. "You've never been with anyone?"

"I've kissed boys before, but no one's ever touched me intimately until you."

His heart hammered in his chest and his hand slid down her body, cupping her between her legs. "I'm the first man to ever touch this sweet pussy?"

She nodded.

The thought that she was untouched made his blood heat. Knowing that only his fingers had traced those slick lips, that only his hand had given her pleasure, made him want her even more. And damn if he didn't want to keep her. He wanted to be her first, her only. A possessiveness he'd never felt with anyone else filled him and he wanted Tessa to be his in every way.

He slipped his hand under her dress and stroked the outside of her panties, feeling how damp they were. Her legs spread further, giving him access. Tessa's chest heaved and her hands curled into fists at her sides. His baby obviously wanted him, and he didn't see any reason to deny her.

"This pussy's wet for me, isn't it?" he asked.

She nodded, licking her lips.

"You want me to make you come again, baby?"

"Please," she begged.

Morgan watched her eyes darken. He eased down onto his knees in front of the couch and reached up to slide her panties down her legs. He bunched the skirt of her dress around her waist and groaned when he saw her slick pussy, the lips dewy from her arousal. He spread her legs further, her pussy opening to him. Her little clit was already hard and peeking out.

Morgan pulled her ass to the edge of the cushions, gripping her cheeks with both hands. Lowering his head, he swiped his tongue against her soft skin, gathering her nectar on his tongue.

"Mm, baby. You taste so damn good."

Tessa whimpered as his tongue stroked her again. Morgan feasted on her, using his lips, teeth, and tongue to drive her desire higher and higher. He circled her clit before sucking it into his mouth, drawing on the little bud long and hard. Tessa bucked under him, nonsensical words spilling from her lips as she tried to push her pussy closer to him. He gave her what she wanted, what she needed. His tongue delved inside her tight channel, flicking in and out, fucking her like he wanted to do with his cock.

She went wild, clawing his shoulders and crying out his name as her release coated his lips. He continued to fuck her with his tongue, feeling her pussy ripple and try to pull him in deeper. When she was panting and limp beneath him, he kissed her sweet lips one more time before pulling away. He wiped her juices from his face and fought the urge to bury himself deep inside of her.

"I love watching you come," he said.

"St-stand up," she said, lifting her back from the couch. She left her dress bunched around her, her legs still spread and that pretty pussy on display.

Morgan rose to his feet, his cock trying to punch through his jeans. Tessa reached for him with shaky hands and unfastened the button on his pants before sliding the zipper down. His heated gaze tracked her movements as she shoved his jeans and boxer briefs down his hips until his cock sprang free. There was already pre-cum beading on the tip, and his cock jerked as she licked her lips again.

"I've never done this before," she admitted. "But I've read a lot of erotic books and I want to try it."

His hand slid into her hair, bringing those sensual lips closer. She opened, her tongue flicking out to lick the drop of cum from the tip. Morgan groaned, his heart racing as her lips parted more and fitted around the head of his cock. His grip on her hair tightened, as he pulled her down his length. She gagged for a second and he pulled back.

"Deep breath, baby."

She sucked in air through her nose and he pushed forward again, until she'd taken all of him. Morgan drew back, then thrust forward again.

"So good," he murmured.

He pumped his hips, his cock surging between those luscious lips. Her hands gripped his hips as he fed her every inch of his cock again and again. Her little tongue flicked the head when he drew back and he groaned, pushing forward again. He fucked her mouth with long, deep strokes until he felt his release building.

"I'm gonna cum, baby. Are you going to be a good girl and swallow it all?"

She moaned and her grip tightened on him.

Morgan thrust faster, harder, until he roared out his release, shooting jets of cum into her mouth and down her throat. When he pulled out, she licked the last droplets from her lips. Fuck if that wasn't the hottest thing he'd ever seen. He could still see her pussy and saw that she was wetter than ever.

His thumb caressed her cheek. "Did you like that?"

"Yes," she said softly.

He grinned. "You're such a naughty girl."

Her cheeks flushed and she smiled up at him almost shyly.

"If you don't cover that pussy, I'm going to make you scream my name again. And next time, I might not stop. Your first time shouldn't be on the living room couch with your dress bunched around your waist."

"I don't care when it is or how I'm dressed, as long as it's with you."

God damn. His dick went hard again.

Morgan stripped off his clothes, wondering if this made him even more of an asshole than he already felt, then reached for her dress, pulling it over her head. Her breasts bounced as they were freed and he groaned when he saw she wasn't wearing a bra. She was a fucking work of art, her body curved in all the right places.

He didn't have a damn condom, even though he'd bought some and stashed them upstairs, and Morgan knew he should use one. Not that he wasn't clean, but if she was a virgin, what were the chances she was on birth control? A vision of Tessa swollen with his child made his balls ache. Even though he knew it was wrong, he was taking her bare. He knew it made him an asshole, and he'd have to beg her forgiveness later, but he'd never wanted anything as badly as he wanted Tessa right now. He fucking wanted to feel every damn inch of her, and he wanted to fill her with his cum, mark her as his.

"I'm going to make you come again, baby, get you nice and loose before we even think about me entering you. Do you want my mouth again or my fingers?" he asked.

"Both," she said breathlessly. "I want your tongue on my clit and your fingers inside me."

The fact she wasn't shy about asking for what she wanted made his dick even harder. Morgan sank to his knees in front of her, spreading her thighs as wide as they would go. He leaned down and flicked her clit with his tongue as his fingers teased her opening. Her hand sifted through his hair as she pulled his mouth tighter against her pussy. Morgan stroked her clit with his tongue as his fingers pumped in and out of her. Her slick walls were so fucking snug he knew she'd squeeze his cock.

He fucked her faster, harder, as his lips and tongue tormented her. Tessa came, pulling his hair as her hips bucked against his mouth. Morgan leaned back as she trembled from the force of her release. He grabbed her hips, his cock throbbing as he slid the head between her slick lips. Once. Twice. He bumped her clit each time, then held her close as he slowly sank inside of her.

She was so fucking tight, just like he knew she'd be, he damn near saw stars. He stroked in and out of her, working his cock inside of her, sliding in another inch each time. He thrust forward, hard and deep, until he filled her completely. She cried out and clung to him.

"I'm sorry, baby. I know it hurts."

She whimpered and bit her lip. Morgan held still, giving her time to adjust to his size. Her hands slid up and down his forearms.

"You can move," she said. "It doesn't hurt anymore."

He took his time, every stroke slow as he pulled nearly all the way out then slid back in. Morgan reached for her clit, rubbing it with his thumb. Tessa moaned and arched her back, thrusting those pretty tits up at him. He leaned down and took one of her hard nipples into his mouth, sucking on it and lightly grazing it with his teeth.

He fucked her harder, faster, driving his cock into her tight channel. Tessa clung to him as she cried out, her pussy clenching him and coating his cock with her cream. Morgan let go, pumping load after load of cum into her, not stopping until every drop had been drained from his balls. He held her close, his cock still buried deep inside of her, and knew that he never wanted to let her go.

She murmured something that sounded almost like *I love you* and Morgan kissed her hard. He withdrew from her sweet body, lifted her into his arms, and carried her upstairs. Morgan eased her down onto his bed, crawled in next to her, and pulled her tight against him. He didn't know what the future held for them, but he knew one thing was for sure. Tessa had already wrapped him around her finger, and he didn't want to imagine his life without her.

Chapter Six

Tessa stretched and smiled. Morgan's half of the bed was empty, and she wondered how long she'd slept. A glance at the window showed the sun had sunk nearly to its lowest point. Her body ached but in the best of ways. When Morgan had said he was bringing her home, she'd never thought she'd end up in his bed so soon, or at all for that matter. She'd hoped it would happen though.

Her thighs were sticky from his cum and she rolled out of bed, heading for the hall bathroom. She ran the hot water until steam billowed out around the curtain then she stepped under the spray, sighing in pleasure. Her muscles loosened and the ache between her legs dulled. Morgan had thoroughly pleased her, and she hoped he planned to do it again. She didn't care if she couldn't walk tomorrow.

Her hand coasted over the angry red scar on her ribs. The sutures had been removed before she'd left the hospital, and the doctor had assured her it was healed but could be tender for another week or two. Another angry red mark marred her stomach, where they'd gone in to stop the internal bleeding. It was mostly healed too. Even though Morgan had pounded her pretty hard, neither of her injuries hurt.

When she was finished with her shower, she pulled on another sundress. In hopes of a repeat of earlier, she left off her bra and panties. It felt decadent going bare beneath the thin dress, and she wondered if Morgan would notice. Looking in the mirror, she smiled as she saw her nipples poking through. That should be enough to tease him. She didn't care if she was sore, she wanted him again and again. It felt like she had a lifetime to make up for, and she wanted every second to count. To think, they could have been together for years now, if only one of them had been brave enough to make the first move.

Her cheeks flushed when she recalled telling him she loved him, but she'd said it so softly she hoped he hadn't heard. Tessa hadn't meant for the words to slip out, but they had just the same. Morgan hadn't said it back, so he either hadn't heard her, or he just didn't feel the same. It hurt her heart to think he couldn't love her back. It still baffled her that he wanted her at all. She was just a poor girl from the wrong side of town, and everyone knew Morgan came from money and had options.

Hell, half the woman in town probably threw themselves at him. She'd seen him out on dates over the years, a perfectly coiffed woman on his arm every time, and probably in his bed later that night. She'd always told herself it didn't matter, that he would never belong to her. But that hadn't stopped her from hurting just the same. Not that she'd ever tell him that. If anything, she'd learned that Morgan could be sensitive and truly cared about other people. If he thought his actions had hurt her, even if she had just been a child, he would probably blame himself and apologize to her. Again.

She didn't want his apology though. She just wanted him.

Tessa made her way downstairs. The doorbell chimed as she reached the bottom. Morgan stepped into the front entry, shutting off the alarm, before opening the door. The scent of Chinese food wafted across the opening and Tessa moved closer, peering out the door at the delivery boy. His eyes widened when he saw her and Morgan turned. His gaze zeroed in on her breasts and slid down her body before he let out a growl. He quickly paid the boy and slammed the door shut, resetting the alarm.

He stalked into the kitchen with her on his heels and he set the sacks on the counter. When he faced her, he looked half wild, his eyes dark and possessive. His gaze scanned her again, pausing on her breasts.

Morgan took a step toward her, then another. She almost felt like she was being stalked by a jungle cat. When he stopped mere inches away, he reached for the top of her dress, pulling it down and freeing her breasts. He stared, his gaze hungry as her nipples hardened even more in the cool air.

He cupped one pert breast and stroked his thumb across her. "These are mine," he said. "And no one should see them but me."

Her eyes widened and her heart raced.

Morgan jerked the skirt of her dress up and plunged two fingers into her wet heat. "*This* is mine."

His fingers pumped in and out of her and Tessa worried her legs would buckle. She'd never seen this side of Morgan before, but she had to admit it was rather hot. She liked the possessive gleam in his eye, the way he was fucking her with his fingers to prove he owned her body.

"No one should see you this way, but me," he said. "When the sunlight came through the door, your dress became transparent and that boy could see everything that belongs to me."

His words sent a shiver down her spine and she wondered if he was going to take her again, right here and now in the kitchen. Part of her really hoped he would.

"Do I need to mark you with my cum again?" he asked, his voice soft as he leaned closer, his lips brushing the shell of her ear. "You gave this sweet pussy to me, gave your innocence to me, and now you're mine. And I don't share, Tessa. Not you. I could never share you."

His fingers slipped from her body and he licked them clean.

"Morgan, I..."

He kissed her, silencing her words. His tongue thrust between her lips, his kiss hard and demanding. It was almost as if he were branding her. The way her body tingled, she knew she'd never want anyone other than Morgan. He was all she'd ever wanted, and now that she'd had a taste, she didn't want to let him go.

"We're going to eat, and then you're going to be a good girl and rest," he said. "But if you ever come to the door like that again, I will fuck you long and hard, fill you up with my cum over and over, until you remember that you're mine."

She moaned, her pussy throbbing with need.

Morgan pulled away, fixing the top of her dress, then turned to wash his hands at the sink. He took out their dinner from the carryout sacks as if nothing had happened. Tessa sank onto a chair at the kitchen table, her legs no longer able to hold her up. Her heart still pounded in her chest and her pussy was slick. She'd thought for sure he'd take her, but he'd backed away, showing he was in control.

As they ate their dinner, she watched him, looking for any sign of the possessive male that she'd seen moments before. But he was back to his usual charming self. The Morgan Hilliard she'd known all her life. If she couldn't still feel his fingers inside of her, she'd wonder if she'd imagined it.

Holy hell! She didn't know where that side of Morgan had come from, but she was damn sure she wanted to see it again. The way he'd looked at her, the commanding way he'd touched her, had been the hottest thing she'd ever seen. Apparently her sweet, mild-mannered vet was hiding a possessive beast inside, and she couldn't wait to see him unleashed again.

Morgan cleared the table after they were finished eating and gently took her by the hand. He led her into the living room and pulled her down onto the couch next to him. The TV clicked on and he put on a random movie, his arm curving around her shoulders and bringing her tight against his side.

"Morgan, do you have to work tomorrow?" she asked.

"Yeah, baby. I have to go in for a full day. I have appointments from opening to close."

"Do you think I could go with you?"

He glanced at her, his gaze concerned. "Maybe you should hang out here and rest tomorrow. I don't want you to overdo it."

Overdo it? He'd fucked her on this very couch just hours ago and he was worried a trip to the clinic would be too much for her?

His nose teased her ear as he leaned in closer. "And if you're really good and rest all day, you may get a reward when I get home."

"A reward?" she asked, more than a little interested.

"I think a day of rest deserves at least an orgasm or two."

Her heart thumped in her chest.

Morgan smiled down at her. "What do you think, sweetheart? Think you can hang out here tomorrow and take it easy?"

She nodded.

Morgan pressed his lips to hers. "Good girl. I

promise it will be worth it."

Tessa sighed and snuggled against him. It sounded like he had no intention of touching her tonight, since he was determined she needed more rest. She'd rested so much in the hospital, the last thing she wanted to do was lie around the house with nothing to do. But she knew Morgan was just looking out for her. He'd offered to take her to the clinic sometime, so even if she didn't go tomorrow, it didn't mean she'd never get out of the house.

She just hoped that the alarm on the house was enough of a deterrent for Trotter. Because if the man figured out she was alone in this house, she didn't doubt for one second that he'd come for her. Trotter might be able to overpower her, but he'd be no match for Morgan, and he likely knew that. Suddenly, she wasn't looking forward to tomorrow quite so much. What good was the promise of orgasms if she was snatched out of the house before she could get them?

Tessa had a really bad feeling about tomorrow. But she didn't want to come across as whiny to the guy she'd been crushing on most of her life. She'd plan to stay here, alone, like he'd asked. But she wouldn't rest easy until Morgan came home from work.

"You have a landline, don't you?" she asked, thinking about her missing cell phone.

"In the kitchen."

"Good."

Morgan squeezed her. "Everything is going to be fine, Tessa."

Famous last words.

* * *

Morgan couldn't stop the smile that stayed on his lips all morning. He'd convinced Tessa to sleep in his bed last night, even though he'd done nothing more than hold her. He'd asked her to move her things into his bedroom while he was at work today, wanting to sleep with her every night while she was under his roof. He just had to figure out how to keep her there, even after the issue with Trotter was resolved.

He'd noticed she seemed nervous about being alone, but he'd been sure to set the alarm before he left. No one was going in or out without the alarm company being notified, and they in turn would call him. He'd given Tessa the code, but cautioned her to remain in the house. The last thing he wanted was for her to feel like a prisoner, but he didn't trust Trotter not to snatch her off the street if she left the safety of his home.

"You're in a good mood," Jeanie said.

"It's a beautiful morning," he said.

She leaned across his desk, setting some files down, and he froze as her top gaped open. It wasn't the first time she'd tried to come onto him, but it was the first time she'd blatantly shown him she wasn't wearing a bra. Morgan jerked his gaze from her breasts and looked up at her. She gave him a slow smile that was probably supposed to encourage him or turn him on. All he could think was that her breasts were nowhere near as luscious as Tessa's.

"That's not very professional," Morgan said.

She pouted. "I thought we were friends, Dr. Hilliard. You're single and I'm single. I don't see the harm in having a little fun. You have a half hour until your first appointment. We could lock the door and…" She bit her lip.

"Jeanie, I'm not interested. You may leave now."

Her eyes flashed with anger. "Not interested? We're close to the same age, we both like working with animals, and I'm damn good in bed."

He sighed wearily, tired of the games the women in town were playing just so they could get their hands on his money.

Jeanie skirted the desk and dropped to her knees. She reached for his pants. "Maybe I just need to show you what you're missing."

He grabbed her wrist before she could curl those fingers into his pants. "Jeanie, if you don't stop, I'm sending you home."

She snorted. "Everyone knows you haven't been seeing anyone. Aren't you tired of fucking your own hand, Morgan? I'll even let you come in my mouth."

His grip tightened a moment and he flung her hand away. "That's it. You're done for the day."

Her cheeks flushed and her lips thinned as she shot to her feet.

There was a knock at his door and his receptionist poked her head through. "Dr. Hilliard, you have a call on line one. It's Tessa. She said you forgot to start the coffee this morning and she can't figure out the coffeemaker."

"Thank you, Vanessa."

The receptionist disappeared and Jeanie glowered at him. "Tessa is at your house?"

He paused, his hand on the phone. "Yes, Tessa is at my house."

"And is she in your bed?" Jeanie asked boldly.

Morgan's eyebrows lifted. "That's none of your concern, or anyone else's. Please close the door behind you on your way out. And I meant what I said. You're done here today."

As Jeanie stormed out of his office, slamming the door so hard it rattled on the hinges, he picked up the phone and pressed the button for line one.

"Morning, sweetheart," he said. "I'm sorry I

forgot about the coffee."

"It's fine. I'm just worried I'm going to break your machine. It's so fancy and there are so many buttons."

He bit his lip and smiled a little. It wasn't that fancy, but it did have more than just an on/off switch. He walked her through the steps for getting a pot brewing, staying on the phone with her while she got a pot going.

"Will you be home for lunch?" she asked.

Morgan pulled up his schedule on the computer. "I must have had a cancellation. It looks like I have a break between one and two. I can come home for a little bit then. Do you want me to pick up something on my way?"

"I know how to cook, Morgan."

"I never said you didn't, baby. I just thought I'd take care of you and bring something with me."

"Morgan, your kitchen is like something out of my dreams. I'd honestly like to make lunch for us. I saw some ground beef in the fridge. What if I make hamburgers? Are there buns here?"

"Check the pantry. If you don't see any, I can get some on my way home."

He heard the pantry door open and listened to her rummage around.

"There's some in here and it looks like they haven't expired yet. They're pretty soft," she said.

"Then it sounds like you're all set. Do you need anything else? I have my first appointment soon, but if you think of anything while I'm with a patient you can leave a message with Vanessa."

"Now that I have coffee, everything is fine."

Morgan smiled. "I'll see you soon, sweetheart." He paused. "I miss you."

"I miss you too, Morgan," she said softly.

Morgan disconnected the call and started preparing for his first appointment. It didn't escape his notice that Pamela Richards was bringing her dog Bubbles in. Again. According to the notes in the file, she was worried that Bubbles was sleeping too much. She'd been in last week because Bubbles wasn't eating enough. A few days before that, she'd come in because she thought Bubbles had been stung by a bee. So far, he hadn't found a damn thing wrong with the dog, and her owner's clothes had been getting tighter and lower cut with every visit. He had a suspicion there was nothing wrong with the dog and Miss Richards was suffering from gold fever.

Blowing out a breath, he grabbed the file off his desk and stepped into the hall. Now that he'd kicked Jeanie out for the day, he didn't have an assistant. Although, he'd much rather deal with his patients without an extra set of hands, than deal with the woman trying to stick her hands down his pants. There was only one set of lips he wanted wrapped around his cock, and that was Tessa's.

Morgan opened the door to the waiting room and smiled at everyone. "Bubbles."

Pamela Richards stood, a skintight dress clinging to her body. The dress had a plunging neckline so low, he worried her breasts might pop out if she bent over. His gaze scanned the others. Some were dressed normally and were apparently there because their pets were really sick. But there were two others who were dressed with seduction on their minds. It was going to be a long fucking day. Maybe he should have brought Tessa after all. They hadn't really discussed where things were going with them, but he'd meant what he said. She was his, and he wasn't letting her go.

Morgan led Miss Richards and Bubbles down the hall to the first exam room. He set the file on the counter and reached down to pick up the Pit Bull mix. She was a sweet girl who was so old she'd lost most of her teeth, and yet she still wiggled when she saw him.

"So Bubbles is sleeping a lot?" Morgan asked as he petted the dog.

"Yes. She just seems to sleep the day away."

"Miss Richards…"

"Pamela," she said, a smile curving her lips. "I think we know each other well enough to be on a first name basis, don't you, Morgan? I can call you Morgan, can't I?"

"Dr. Hilliard is fine," he said.

She pursed her lips.

"I'm going to take some blood samples and run a few tests, but I suspect Bubbles is just old and tired, Miss Richards. She's fifteen now, and while she still gets around well, she may not be with us for much longer."

"Bubbles and I appreciate everything you do for us," Miss Richards said. She reached across the exam table and placed her hand on his arm, giving his biceps a squeeze. "Oh my, Dr. Hilliard. You do fill out a lab coat rather well."

Morgan pulled out of her grip and took a syringe out of the cabinet. He took a few vials of blood from Bubbles, poor dog, and then eased the older canine back onto the floor.

"I should have the results in a day or two," he told Miss Richards. "Vanessa will call you."

Miss Richards bit her lip in what was probably supposed to be a coy move, but it just irritated Morgan. "You won't call me? I do so love to hear from you."

Morgan decided being blunt was the best way to

handle the tenacious woman. "Miss Richards, you're a pretty lady, but I'm not interested. For both my sake and Bubbles', please stop setting appointments just so you can flirt with me. It takes up space from someone who might really need the appointment."

Irritation flashed across her face, only to be replaced with a simpering smile.

"Dr. Hilliard, perhaps we could go to dinner tonight? I'd really love to get to know you better, and I think we'd have a lot in common."

"I have plans."

"A date?" she asked, a bit of bite to her tone.

Vanessa popped her head into the exam room. "Sorry to bother you, Dr. Hilliard, but Tessa called again. She asked if you would stop by the store on your way home to get some tea."

Morgan smiled at her. "Tell Tessa I will be happy to get tea for her. Ask her what kind she wants and make a note of it for me."

Vanessa nodded and ducked back out of the room.

Miss Richards turned a frosty glare his way. Tessa had impeccable timing. He wondered if he could convince her to interrupt all of his appointments today. Or maybe he'd just start each visit with a disclaimer that there was a woman living in his house.

"Tessa Milner?" Miss Richards asked. "That two-bit whore is staying in your house?"

Morgan felt his face flush with anger as his hands clenched at his sides. "Excuse me?"

"She's trash, Dr. Hilliard. I'm sure she spreads her legs easily, but you can do much better."

Morgan had never been so tempted to hit a woman in his life.

"Miss Richards, your visit is over. I would

suggest you find another vet to see in the future. And if you so much as breathe in Tessa's direction, you will have me to deal with. If anyone in this scenario is a whore, it's you."

She gasped and tightened her hand on Bubbles' leash and took off out of the room like the devil was nipping at her heels. Morgan wiped a hand down his face and wondered how many more insane women he would have to deal with for the day. None of them had given him so much as a second glance until they found out he was rich. Gold diggers, every single one.

Morgan dropped Bubbles' vials into the lab drop box, made some notes in her file, then left it in the outgoing box. He stopped by his office to get the next patient's file, thankful the owner was a male. Unless Brett Foster had started batting for the other team, the visit shouldn't have any surprises.

Chapter Seven

Tessa mixed the ground beef with diced onions, Worcestershire sauce, an egg, and some garlic powder. Her hands were goopy as she kneaded the mixture in a large bowl, humming to a tune in her head. She'd put on another sundress, but had been a good girl and wore panties this time, and her bare feet danced along the tile floor as she shimmied in place. Morgan would be home soon, and she couldn't wait to see him.

She shaped the patties and placed them in the large skillet she'd found. While they cooked, she took out a head of lettuce and a tomato, slicing both to garnish the burgers. Tessa flipped the patties and added a thick slice of cheddar to the tops of them while they finished cooking.

She'd found a bag of frozen fries and heated them in the oven. They were already cooling on the back of the stove. By the time she was putting the hamburgers together, she heard the front door open and the alarm go off. She tensed until she heard the code being punched in.

"Tessa!" Morgan called out.

"In the kitchen!" she yelled back.

She heard the door close and the alarm being reset. When Morgan stepped into the kitchen, she stopped to stare a moment. He set down a jug of sweet tea and gave her a sexy smirk, folding his arms over his chest, making his biceps bulge.

"Damn, Dr. Hilliard. You make scrubs look good."

He chuckled and came toward her, wrapping an arm around her waist and kissing her cheek. "And you make me want to do very bad things. If I'd known how good you'd look in these sundresses, that's all I would have bought for you."

"I'm afraid this is the last one until I wash clothes. You'll have to settle for seeing me in pants the next day or two."

"Pants have their advantages," he said, sliding his hand down to her ass, giving it a squeeze. "Like the way they highlight one of your best features."

Her panties grew damp and she clenched her thighs together. All it took was one touch and she went up in flames. She moved away from him and took their plates to the table. While Morgan sat, she fetched the tea from the counter and poured them each a glass. As a true Southern girl, she should have made her own, but she'd wanted something quick and easy for today.

She placed the glasses on the table and took a seat next to him.

Morgan took a bite and moaned. "These are really good, baby."

Tessa smiled.

"Were you planning to cook dinner or did you want me to grab something?" he asked. "I have some steaks thawing in the fridge, but they might not be ready until tomorrow."

"I don't mind cooking," she said. "I'll look through the fridge and pantry and throw something together."

They finished eating and Morgan pushed away from the table, pulling her onto his lap. Tessa looped her arms around his neck and kissed him softly.

Morgan's hand slid up her leg, climbing higher and higher. When his fingers teased her panties, Tessa trembled.

"Have you been thinking about me today?" he asked.

"Every second you've been gone."

He rubbed the satin material. "These are awfully wet, baby."

"That's what happens when you turn me on."

He smiled a little. "And how did I turn you on this time?"

"You grabbed my ass."

Morgan chuckled. "I'll have to remember that."

"Do you have to leave soon?"

He looked at the clock on the wall. "In about twenty minutes."

Tessa licked her lips. "Then we have just enough time."

He cocked an eyebrow at her and she stood up, sliding her panties down her legs and kicking them away. Morgan watched her with a heated gaze as she reached for his scrubs, pulling his pants down far enough to free his cock. Tessa placed a hand on his shoulder and straddled him, sinking onto his hard length until he filled her all the way.

She threw back her head and moaned as she rode him. Morgan pulled the top of her dress down and latched onto one of her nipples. He sucked hard then released it with a *pop*. Morgan leaned further back in his chair and lifted her dress.

"Beautiful," he murmured as he watched her pussy slide down over his cock again and again.

"Touch me, Morgan. I'm so close."

He reached between them and rubbed her clit with his thumb, slow tight circles that had her clutching at his shoulders and riding him harder. Her release nearly took her breath away and Morgan gripped her hips, thrusting up into her several times, his cum bathing the inside of her. Tessa shuddered in his arms as she caught her breath. Her pussy throbbed from the force of her orgasm and she wished they could stay like this a while.

Morgan pushed their plates away and lifted her, setting her on the edge of the table. Her legs were splayed on either side of him and he bunched her skirt around her waist. His finger traced over her slit and he bit his lip.

"Damn but I love seeing my cum on you." He leaned forward to lick her nipple again. "Mine."

"Yours," she agreed.

Morgan gathered the cum on his fingers and plunged them inside of her, stroking her several times. "Don't wash this off. I want to know that you're marked as mine the rest of the day."

His words turned her on again and she wished he didn't have to go back to work. Morgan sucked at her nipples again then seemed reluctant to pull away. He fixed the top of her dress and stared at her pussy with a hungry expression. With a sigh, he stood and helped her off the table.

Morgan tucked his cock back into his pants then kissed Tessa long and deep. "I'll be home after five."

"I'll be anxiously waiting."

Morgan smiled and kissed her once more before heading back to the clinic. She smiled. He might want his cum to remain on her all day, but it hadn't escaped her notice he hadn't cleaned up, which meant hers was still on his cock. She wondered if he'd done it on purpose.

The man was going to drive her crazy.

Tessa cleaned up the kitchen and peered out the front window. A dark car was parked at the curb, one she'd seen too many times before. Her heart pounded in her chest and she wondered if Stan Trotter was staring at her through the dark windows. Fear froze her in place. She dropped the curtain, but they were too gauzy to hide that horrible black car from view.

The rear door of the car opened and the rotund Stan Trotter got out. He approached the front door as if he were merely taking a Sunday stroll. The bell rang, but Tessa wasn't about to answer it. No way in hell was she letting that man in the house.

A fist pounded on the door making it rattle. "Tessa, open up. It's time to end this nonsense and come home."

"I am home," she called out.

"You better hope that vet hasn't touched you because I paid top price for that virgin pussy of yours. It's mine and I plan to claim it."

A chill skirted down her spine.

"Tessa, you're mine. You've always been mine. Remember all the times your daddy let me come in your room? You miss my touch, don't you, sweet girl? I was only biding my time until you were a little older, a little riper."

"I'm not going anywhere with you. I don't belong to you, Mr. Trotter."

He chuckled. "I know just how tight that little pussy is going to be, Tessa, and I plan to be the first one inside of it. I'm going to fuck you as many times as I want."

Bile rose in her throat at the thought of him touching her in any way.

"And when I'm done with you, when I've loosened you up enough, I have just the place for you," he said.

Tessa trembled from head to toe and her knees felt weak. She told herself she was safe, the alarm was on, and Morgan had assured her that no one was going to take her from his house.

"Just think about it, dear," Trotter said. "You can

either come to me willingly, or I can make life very difficult for your little vet. Maybe I'll even let him have you when I'm done. If you think he'd still want you after I let all of my men fuck you."

Tessa bolted for the bathroom and threw up. Sobs wracked her body as she clung to the toilet. She'd known Stan Trotter was an evil, vile man, but to hear what he planned to do to her... She stayed in the bathroom, too afraid to leave the small space. Her tears eventually dried up and she leaned against the bathroom wall, her knees pressed to her chest.

Morgan found her hours later.

He froze in the bathroom doorway and slowly eased into the room, kneeling in front of her, smoothing her hair out of her face. "Honey, what's wrong?"

"Trotter was here," she said in a listless voice. "He wanted to make sure I knew I belonged to him."

"What did he say, Tessa?"

Her eyes filled with tears again. "He told me how he was going to use me, then give me to his men. He said maybe when they were done he'd give me back to you."

Morgan cursed and pulled her into his arms, rubbing her back. "Baby, I'm not going to let that happen."

"There's nothing you can do to stop him, Morgan. He thinks I belong to him and he won't stop until he has me. Now that he knows for sure that I'm here, it will only be a matter of time before he finds a way around your security system."

Morgan lifted her into his arms and carried her out of the bathroom and up to his bedroom. He eased her down on the bed and disappeared into the master bath. He came back a minute later with a cold, wet rag in his hands, using it to wipe her face, then folded it and pressed it against the back of her neck. "What exactly did he say to you, Tessa?" Morgan asked. "I know you don't want to think about it, but it's important."

"He said my virgin pussy was his and he was going to use me long and hard."

Morgan's jaw clenched.

"Morgan, if he takes me and finds out I'm not a virgin, what's he going to do to me?"

"We're not ever going to find out. Tessa… you like being here with me, right? We have fun together and we get along well."

She nodded.

"And you like sleeping in my bed at night?" he asked.

"Of course, Morgan. I don't want to go with him. I want to stay here with you."

"What if we made our arrangement a more permanent one? I can't promise it would make Trotter back off, but if he knew you belonged to me, then maybe he would lose interest."

"Morgan, I don't know what you're talking about. Permanent? You mean like move in here?"

He smiled a little. "Baby, in case you hadn't noticed, you've already moved in here. And since my staff at the clinic now know that you're here, and Trotter apparently figured it out, it's only a matter of time before everyone knows we're living together. Even if they don't know if it's temporary or not."

"Then what…"

"Marry me," he said.

Tessa's eyes went wide.

"Tessa… I wasn't kidding when I said you're mine. I've never felt possessive of anyone before, but I think you bring out the caveman in me." He grinned a little. "While I love marking you with my cum, I'd like to claim you in a way everyone can see. Wear my ring. Be my wife."

"Morgan, I..." She bit her lip. She wanted to say yes, so very much. But what if he was wrong about Trotter? What if their marriage pushed him over the edge and he came after Morgan?

His eyes darkened. "You're going to say yes, Tessa. You know you want to."

"How do you know I'll say yes?" she asked.

"Because if I have to I will fuck you all night long until you're mindless with pleasure and agree to anything I say."

She snorted. "If that's supposed to be a threat, it's a poor one. I love feeling you inside of me."

Morgan leaned forward and kissed her, his teeth grazing her bottom lip. "Say yes," he whispered against her lips.

"Yes," she said softly.

Morgan grinned then kissed her harder.

"When are we getting married?" she asked.

"I don't have any appointments tomorrow until after nine. We'll get up in the morning and go to the courthouse to apply for a license."

"How long does that take?"

Morgan shrugged. "I've never wanted to marry someone before so I'm not sure. As soon as we have our license, we'll get married. I don't trust the judge so we'll find a minister."

"Morgan, are you sure you want to marry me? I can live here with you without you having to give me your name."

He rubbed a hand across her belly. "I can't keep my hands off you, Tessa, and as you've noticed, I like the way you look with my cum on you and in you. You're going to end up pregnant sooner or later, and I'd rather we be married when that happens. I'm not just grasping at straws, baby. This isn't something I would offer to just any woman. I want you to be mine, in every way possible."

"I want that too."

Morgan kissed her, his lips traveling from her mouth to her jaw. Then he lightly nipped her on the ear. "Now that that's settled, were you a good girl earlier? Did you do what I said?"

"Wh-what you said?"

He pulled up her dress and smiled. "Good, you didn't get cleaned up."

"Morgan, as much of a turn-on as it is that you like seeing yourself on me, your slight obsession is a little weird."

"You get turned on by wearing my cum?" he asked.

Tessa rolled her eyes. "That's what you got out of that sentence?"

Morgan kissed her then lifted her dress over her head. Her nipples hardened under his gaze and she felt herself getting wet. The man was insatiable, but so was she. Morgan stripped out of his scrubs, his cock already hard.

"Get on your knees, baby."

Tessa slid off the side of the bed and fell to her knees.

"You liked sucking my cock, didn't you?" he asked.

"Very much."

He held his dick and painted her lips with the pre-cum on the tip. Tessa licked it off, drawing a groan from Morgan. He fisted her hair and she opened her mouth. Morgan thrust inside, his cock sliding along her tongue until he hit the back of her throat.

"Relax, baby. Let me in all the way," he murmured.

She took a breath and he slid in further. He pumped his hips, the grip on her hair tightening. Her hands settled on his hips as he fucked her mouth, pulling her down his length with every thrust. She hollowed her cheeks, sucking him hard.

"Fuck, baby. You're going to swallow it all, aren't you?"

She hummed and kept sucking.

Morgan thrust harder until his cum was spurting into her mouth. Tessa swallowed everything he gave her, but his grip didn't loosen. He kept plunging between her lips even after the last drop had hit her tongue. After a few more pumps of his hips, he released her and pulled free of her mouth.

Morgan picked her up and tossed her onto the bed, making her giggle.

"Spread those legs and show that pretty pussy to me."

Tessa's heart hammered in her chest as she parted her legs.

He caressed her inner thighs, pushing them wider apart, and settled between them, his breath fanning across her. The first flick of his tongue had her gasping and fighting to hold still. He lapped at her folds, his tongue teasing her clit. Tessa lifted her hips, pressing closer to his mouth. Pleasure rolled over her in waves as his tongue dipped inside of her, thrusting in and out of her pussy. "Morgan," she moaned.

His tongue delved deeper, harder. He pressed his thumb to her clit and rubbed until she shattered, screaming out his name. Morgan kept rubbing, kept fucking her with his tongue, not letting up until she'd come a second time. He looked satisfied as he crawled up her body. His cock brushed against her and then he plunged inside, stretching and filling her.

Morgan braced a hand on her hip, fucking her hard and deep. His body slapped against hers in a frantic tempo. She stared into his eyes as he came inside of her. Morgan kept pumping, reaching between them to rub her clit. Even though he'd already come, he was still hard, and driving into her like a man possessed. She placed her hand over his, feeling his wet fingers working her clit, then her hand slid a little further. Her fingertips grazed his cock as it thrust in and out of her.

"Christ, Tessa! I'm going to come again," he said, pumping harder and deeper.

Tessa gave herself up to the incredible sensations rolling through her. She came with his name on her lips and her pussy milking every drop of cum from his balls. Morgan stilled inside of her, his pelvic bone pressed tight against her clit.

"I have never met a woman like you before," he said. "You make me wish my cock could just live inside of you."

He slid out then back in, even though he wasn't as hard as before.

"I wouldn't complain," she said.

"I'm putting a ring on your finger," he said. "And then I'm fucking you every chance I get until we make a baby. I'll fuck you long, hard, and deep, in every damn room in the house, and I'm going to fill up this pussy with my cum over and over again. No one will ever doubt who you belong to."

Tessa pulled him down for a kiss, wanting that so damn much. All she'd ever wanted was to feel

Morgan inside of her, to have his arms around her. And now everything she'd ever dreamed of was going to come true.

Chapter Eight

It had been three blissful weeks since Morgan had married Tessa, and he couldn't have been happier. Well, at home anyway. At work was another matter. Jeanie wasn't taking his marriage so well and had let him know countless times what a mistake it was to marry trash like Tessa. Apparently, she'd been running her mouth to his clients as well, and Vanessa had let him know that people weren't happy with his assistant.

He signed the bottom of Jeanie's release papers and stared at her across his desk. He'd called her in, saying he needed to talk to her, and he doubted she was going to take the news of her imminent release very well. Her lips were pursed and fire flashed in her eyes. He'd put up with her nonsense long enough, and hoped he was doing the right thing.

"I know you have it in your head that for some reason I was going to marry you," he told her, "but that would have never happened."

"We make far more sense than you and that penniless whore."

His jaw tightened. "Tessa is not a whore."

"Oh, please. Everyone knows that baby is Stan Trotter's."

The room spun for a moment. "Baby?"

Jeanie smirked. "She didn't tell you? Everyone knows she ordered a pregnancy test from the pharmacy this morning. Word has already spread all over town."

Tessa thought she was pregnant and hadn't told him?

"Stan Trotter's been telling everyone how he used to visit Tessa in her room when she lived with her daddy. Ben Milner let him do whatever he wanted to Tessa. There's no doubt that brat is his and she's just trying to pawn it off as yours."

A red haze covered Morgan's vision. "Stan Trotter used to visit her in her room?"

"Of course. A girl like that gets around."

Morgan was shaking with fury as he handed the discharge papers to Jeanie. "You're fired. Get the hell out of my clinic and don't come back."

Her jaw dropped. "Fired?"

"Yes, fired. Stop spreading malicious lies about my wife. I'm sick of it and so are the clients. If I hear you've said one more negative thing about Tessa, I'll slap you with a defamation lawsuit so fast your head will spin."

Jeanie's jaw snapped shut and she snatched the paper from his hand before storming out of the office. Morgan stuck his head into the hall and called out for Vanessa. When his receptionist hurried into his office, she looked worried.

"Is Jeanie going to cause problems?" Vanessa asked.

"Possibly, but I had another question for you. Have you heard rumors about Stan Trotter and my wife?"

Her cheeks flushed. "He's been telling everyone that he had her first, that he took her innocence at her daddy's house when she was just a kid."

"Vanessa, would you please ask the sheriff to come here? And tell my patients I'll be with them shortly."

"Yes, Dr. Hilliard."

He knew it was a lie that Trotter had taken Tessa's innocence, but the town didn't. He wondered if they might have finally found the ammunition they needed against Ben Milner to get him to talk. Morgan hated that the town was talking about his wife, and saying such horrible things about her. He'd set the record straight, but first he had a snake to catch. And then he was going to find out why his wife hadn't told him she might be pregnant.

Vanessa came back to his office, biting her lip. "Um, Dr. Hilliard, the sheriff can't come right now. He's... he's at your house."

"My house?"

She nodded. "Tessa called the sheriff when Stan Trotter showed up."

Morgan bolted out of his chair. "Cancel my afternoon appointments."

He shrugged off his lab coat and grabbed his keys before dashing out the door. When he pulled up at his house, two deputies had Stan Trotter face down in the yard with his arms behind his back. Morgan barely put the car into park before he was running for the front door. Trotter was yelling obscenities as the deputies cuffed him and hauled him off to a waiting sheriff's department vehicle.

Morgan heard voices in the kitchen and hurried in that direction. "Tessa!"

"In here, Morgan," she called back.

He found her sitting at the kitchen table with the sheriff. She looked a little pale and he noticed her hands were shaking. Morgan knelt at her side, cupping her cheek with his hand.

"Are you all right?"

She nodded. "I'm fine."

"What happened?" Morgan asked.

"Your wife called us when Mr. Trotter showed up on the lawn screaming at her through the closed door. Apparently, he heard that Tessa had bought a pregnancy test this morning. Congratulations, by the way. The thought of her carrying your baby set him off in the worst way," the sheriff said.

Morgan stared down at his wife. "We're going to talk about the pregnancy part of the equation later."

Her cheeks flushed.

Morgan looked back at the sheriff. "Why are you arresting him? Is it something that's going to stick?"

"We have him for trespassing right now. Tessa mentioned he was here before and told me some of the things he said to her. Combined with the malicious crap he's been spewing around town about her, I think we can hold him for a little while."

"Sheriff," Tessa said. "Our neighbor, Ms. Williams, was out walking her dog when Stan first showed up. She may have heard him when he said I was his because he'd paid for me. He said he gave my daddy cold hard cash and owned me."

The sheriff talked to one of his deputies on the radio and asked them to check into it once Trotter was secured.

"I know you've kept Tessa pretty much locked up in this house, but I think it's safe for her to wander around town again on her own," the sheriff said. "I'll hold Trotter as long as I can and try to find more charges. I don't think he'll send anyone after her unless he's confident he's going to be released. And since he's come here twice in person, it could be he doesn't trust anyone to snatch her for him."

"He used to frequent the Golden Apple," Tessa said. "I saw him go into the back with the girls all the time. Maybe he was getting more than a lap dance. The owner sometimes forces the girls to do more than what their job description says. It's not their fault though. They either comply or get fired."

"It's worth looking into." The sheriff stood. "I'm going to see if I can get Ben to crack and tell us everything. In the meantime, I think you two have some celebrating to do."

The sheriff let himself out and Morgan held Tessa's hand. "Is he right? Do we have something to celebrate?"

A small smile crossed her lips. "The test was positive."

Morgan smiled so big his cheeks hurt as he lifted Tessa into his arms, kissing her soundly. "This doesn't change anything. You should still take the test for your G.E.D."

"I've been studying the test guide you bought for me and I think I'm about ready."

"You know I'll support you, no matter what you decide to do, but if you think you might like to train to be a vet tech, it seems I have an opening at the clinic."

"I love you, Morgan, and I love animals, but I don't really want to work with them. Not like that."

"What if I offered Vanessa a promotion if she passes the certification classes and you take the receptionist position?" he asked. "The area behind the desk is big enough to fit a playpen back there, if you wanted to bring the baby to work with you."

"I'll think about it."

"What do you want to do? I've taken the rest of the day off."

"Would you take me to see my dad?"

Morgan was surprised by her request. "You want to go to the jail and see your dad?"

"Yes. Maybe seeing me will make him tell the sheriff the truth. I want to talk to my dad and let him know that despite his best efforts, he didn't ruin my life."

"All right. Let me change and we'll go see your dad."

Morgan pulled off his scrubs, rinsed off in the shower, and put on some jeans and a T-shirt. He wasn't thrilled about Tessa seeing the man who had sold her to a monster, but he wouldn't stop her. He never wanted to get in her way, even if he didn't like the choice she was making. She was a grown woman and could make her own decisions.

When he finished getting ready, they drove over to the jail. Tessa seemed nervous, but if she was determined to do this, Morgan was going to stand by her side. A deputy led them to a table in the visitors' area and they sat and waited. Ben Milner was led over to them a short while later, his wrists shackled in front of him. He looked haggard, his skin a sickly shade.

"Hi, Daddy," Tessa said.

"What are you doing here?" Ben asked.

"I came to see you," Tessa said. "You've been here a month now. I should have come sooner."

"No, you shouldn't have. You shouldn't be here now." Ben's eyes watered. "I was the world's worst father. The things I did, the things I said. Your momma would have been so ashamed of me. I've had some time to sober up in here, and I know the things I did were wrong."

"I wanted you to know that everything turned out all right," Tessa said. "I'm married to Dr. Hilliard, and we're going to have a baby."

Ben's eyes brightened a little. "A baby? I'm going to be a grandfather?"

Morgan tried not to wince at the thought.

"Daddy, Stan Trotter came to the house today. He was calling me names and saying I belonged to him."

Ben seemed to age within minutes. "I've done some truly horrible things all so I could get my hands on alcohol, but I suppose that was the worst. I should have never taken money and agreed to give you to him."

"So you did sell your daughter to Trotter?" Morgan asked.

"Yes," Ben said. "I did."

"Daddy, I know you'll get in even more trouble for admitting that, but would you tell the sheriff? It's the only way to put Trotter away. I don't want him coming after me and my baby."

Ben reached across the table and placed his hands over Tessa's. "I've done wrong by you since your momma died. I guess it's time I did something right. I'll tell the sheriff everything he wants to know."

Morgan saw the tears gathered in Tessa's eyes and knew that she loved her dad, no matter how many horrible things he'd done to her over the years.

"Mr. Milner, why don't you let me get a lawyer for you? Before you talk to the sheriff, you should have some counsel. Maybe you can get a lighter sentence for your testimony," Morgan said.

Ben shook his head. "Won't matter. My liver's shot from all the drinking. I won't live long enough to get out of prison. I need to do this for my daughter. For my grandchild. I need to make things right."

Tears fell down Tessa's cheeks. "I love you, Daddy."

"I love you too, Tessa. I always have. I'm sorry I lost my way after your momma died. I'm real glad you have Dr. Hilliard to take care of you now."

"I love your daughter, Mr. Milner. She'll be well taken care of. Both her and the baby."

"Maybe… maybe one day, if you tell that baby

about their grandpa, you can tell them about the good days. Tessa, I know the house isn't much, but I'm going to sign it over to you. You can do whatever you want with it, but there's a box on the top shelf of my closet. You'll want that."

"All right, Daddy."

A deputy appeared at Ben's side. "Mr. Milner, it's time to go."

"Don't come back here," Ben said. "You live your life, Tessa. Make every day count."

As Ben was led away, Tessa wept in Morgan's arms. His heart was breaking for her. Ben had finally gotten sober only to tell his daughter that he'd never see her again. Morgan led her out of the jail and back to their car. He wrapped his arms around her and held her tight, letting her cry.

"I'm sorry, baby," Morgan said. "I know that was hard."

"Do you think we could go get that box?" she asked as she dried her tears.

"We'll go right now."

Morgan helped her into the car and drove to Tessa's old home. He hadn't told her, but he'd had the furniture and carpets thrown out. The house still smelled of urine and would need to be refinished before it could be sold, if that was what Tessa decided to do with it. She led the way to her father's bedroom and pointed to the box on the top shelf of the closet. Morgan pulled it down.

"Why don't we open it at home?" Morgan suggested. "You probably shouldn't be around this smell for very long."

Tessa nodded and Morgan placed the box in the back of the car and drove home. When they reached their house, he set the box down on the kitchen table and stood back, giving Tessa room. Whatever was inside was meant for her. She carefully opened the flaps and her hand shook as she reached inside.

A gold frame was clutched in her hand and she pulled it out of the box. Tessa bit her lip and more tears slipped down her cheeks. "I thought he'd gotten rid of all of them," she said.

Morgan looked over her shoulder. "Is that your mom? You look like her."

"Yeah. Wasn't she beautiful?"

"Very," Morgan said, pressing a kiss to her temple.

Tessa set the picture aside and pulled out a photo album, filled with pictures of her childhood, when things had been happy in her home. There were other items in the box, including her mother's wedding band. After Tessa looked over everything, she placed it all back into the box, except the picture of her mother. That she carried into the living room and placed on a shelf.

"There was a nice picture in the album of the three of you," Morgan said. "Maybe we can take the photo over to the photo shop and they can blow it up so we can frame it."

"I'd really like that."

Morgan cupped her cheek. "I meant what I said to your dad, Tessa. I love you. I think I've loved you for a long time, even if I could never admit it to myself."

"I love you too. So much."

Morgan kissed her, slowly, softly. He cherished the woman in his arms and would be grateful every day that she was his. Morgan vowed to show his family daily how much he loved them, and he would always put them first. Tessa was his life, and he couldn't wait to raise a family with her. But even more, he wanted to help her realize her dreams, because she'd made all of his come true.

Epilogue

Three years later

"Benjamin Patrick Hilliard, you drop that right now! That's not yours!" Tessa yelled as she marched across the clinic toward their son, her belly looking like it might burst at any moment with their second child.

Their son grinned, squeezing the puppy tight in his arms, as he took off on chubby little legs. Morgan supposed he should step in and save the boy. After all, the puppy really *was* his. Tessa just didn't know it yet.

"You haven't told her?" Marnie Potts asked in a whisper. The pup was part of a litter her Basset Hound had eight weeks ago and they were ready for homes.

"I'm getting around to it," Morgan said.

"You better get to it faster before your son bursts into tears. Assuming Tessa is able to pry that pup out of his hands. He doesn't seem to want to let go."

Morgan chuckled and walked over to his family.

"Tessa, sweetheart. Let Ben hang onto the puppy."

"But it's not his. Marnie only brought them in for a checkup."

"Well, that's mostly true," Morgan said.

Tessa planted her hands on her hips and glared at him. "*Mostly* true? Morgan Hilliard, did you promise your son that puppy?"

Morgan rubbed the back of his neck. "How much trouble will I be in if I say yes?"

Tessa huffed and rolled her eyes. "I swear I'm not raising one child but two. In case it escaped your notice, I'm due any day now. I don't have time to take care of a puppy."

"Baby, I'll take care of the puppy. It will be good for Ben. He's been asking for a puppy since last

Christmas."

"Fine. But I'm not cleaning up any puddles."

Morgan kissed her softly. "You should sit down and rest. Ben can help me in the exam room. Vanessa will help keep an eye on him."

Tessa looked conflicted and glanced at the reception desk. She'd taken the job at his clinic, like he'd hoped, after she'd gotten her G.E.D. Vanessa had passed her vet tech certification classes with flying colors and had stepped into Jeanie's old position. But now, with Tessa so close to delivering, a fresh face sat at reception and he could tell his wife wasn't happy about it.

"She's just temporary," Morgan assured Tessa.

"But what if I can't come back after the baby is born? Two kids will be a lot to handle on top of everything else here."

"If you want to keep working, we'll figure it out, baby. We always do."

She nodded and then paled. A moment later, a puddle flooded the floor at her feet. "Um, Morgan. Do you think Vanessa would watch Ben for a little while? Like maybe long enough for me to deliver this baby?"

Morgan started barking out orders and rushed Tessa to the car. He broke every speed limit in town on his way to the hospital. Tessa remained calm, while his nerves felt like they were shot. She'd pre-registered at the hospital and the nurses smiled warmly at her when they walked through the doors.

"I'm here to have a baby," Tessa said.

"Her water broke about fifteen minutes ago," Morgan said.

Tessa gave them her information and she was settled into a wheelchair and taken to the maternity ward. Morgan helped her into a gown and the nurses fussed over her as she got settled in the bed. Her hand clamped down tight on his with every contraction, but she never complained.

It took three hours before Nicole Elaine Hilliard was placed in her mother's arms. Morgan couldn't remember ever seeing a more beautiful sight and kissed both baby and momma. His heart was full, and he knew life was about as perfect as it would ever get. He had a beautiful family, a thriving business, but most importantly, he had the love of a beautiful woman. Tessa had once told him that he was her hero, but really, she was the one who had saved him. She'd brought love and laughter into his life.

"I love you, Morgan Hilliard," she said, pressing her lips to his.

"And I love you, Tessa Hilliard. I would give the world to you if I could."

Tessa smiled at him warmly. "You already have."

Paige Warren

Paige Warren is a contemporary romance author who believes in happily-ever-after for everyone. Sexy, steamy stories about mobsters, cowboys, inked bad boys, and interracial couples… sometimes with a bit of kink. If you like alpha heroes and strong heroines, then you're in the right place! No matter the odds, in a Paige Warren book, true love conquers all.

When her husband, children, and furbabies aren't demanding her attention, she's typically either writing or reading. Paige enjoys reading a variety of genres from young adult books, to general fiction, and of course, romances! But when it comes to movies, she's a big-time horror fan -- especially the '80s slasher flicks. That being said, ghostly movies are her favorite regardless of when they were made, like Rose Red or The Amityville Horror.

Paige at Changeling: changelingpress.com/ paige-warren-a-202

ChangelingPress.com

Changeling Press publishes Contemporary Women's Fiction, Paranormal Women's Fiction, Action Adventure, Romantic Comedy, Sci-Fi Futuristic, Dark Fantasy, Urban Fantasy, and Cyber-Punk Romance, including MC Romance, Medical Romance, Military, Veterans, and First Responder Romance, Organized Crime, Rock Star Romance, New Adult, Single Parent, Pregnancy, LGBTQA+, Sex/Gender Shifters & Mpreg Romance, Steampunk, Vampire, Werewolf, Shifter, and Zombie Romance.

Formats: Ebooks, Print books, and Audio books

Available at: ChangelingPress.com, Amazon, Apple Books, Barnes & Noble, Kobo, Scribd, Smashwords, and other retail sites.

ChangelingPress.com